Her Benny

Published by The Bluecoat Press, Liverpool
Book design by MARCH Graphic Design Studio, Liverpool
Printed and bound by Grafo

ISBN 9781904438533

Her Benny

Silas Hocking

THE BLUECOAT PRESS

CHAPTER I

Brother and Sister

Perhaps while in our glowing grate
The cheerful blaze is rising higher
There's someone sitting desolate
Without a spark of fire.

Oh, what are we, that God hath blessed
Our winter homes and made them glad,
While other hearts are sore distressed,
While other homes are sad?

IT was getting dark, though the Town Hall clock had only just struck four. But a fog had hung all over Liverpool since morning, and everything was as damp and dismal as it well could be; and now, as evening came on, the fog had settled into a downright drizzle, converting the streets into what seemed to Nelly Bates (who was crouched in the shadow of St. George's Church) to be endless puddles.

"I wish Benny would come," said she to herself. "I wonder what has kept him? He said he'd be here when the clock struck four."

And she wrapped her tattered clothes more closely around her, and looked eagerly down Lord Street and up and down Castle Street. But no Benny appeared in sight.

"I'm glad as how they's lightin' the lamps, anyhow. It'll make it feel a bit warmer, I reckon," she went on, "for it's terrible cold. But Benny won't be long now, nohow. I hope he's sold all his fusees."

And she looked wistfully at the unsold matches lying in her lap. Then, after a pause, she went on again, "I's had desp'rate bad luck today. I reckon the gen'lmen thinks it too much trouble to take off their gloves to get at the coppers. I wonder if they know what it is to be cold and hungry like me?"

And the child moved a little farther into the shadow of the church, to escape the keen cold blast that swept up from the river.

Little Nelly Bates was a delicate-looking child, with a pale, thoughtful face, and big, round, dreamy-looking eyes. She had none of that wolfish expression that so often characterises the street Arabs of our large towns and cities; but, on the contrary, there was an air of refinement about her that was difficult to account for. Poor little waif! Her own mother she could not remember. She had only known a stepmother – a cruel, drunken woman; and, alas! her father was no better. Almost as soon as she could walk she had been sent into the streets with her brother Benny, who was a year older, to get her living as best she could. Never knowing a parent's love, the affections of these two children had gone out to each other. Each to each was more than all the world beside. At the time our story opens Nelly was nine years of age, and Benny, as we said, a year older.

Still the minutes dragged along, and Benny came not. The 'busses were crowded with people outside and in, wrapped in huge warm overcoats, and all down Lord Street she watched the hurrying crowds bending their steps homewards. And she tried to picture their cheerful homes, with great blazing fires, and happy children running to greet them, and wondered how none of them ever paused to

5

notice her, shivering there in the shadow of the church.

At length the great clocks all around began to strike five, and Benny had not come; a sense of unutterable loneliness crept over the child, and she began to cry. Besides, she was hungry and cold, and there was a great fear in her heart that something had befallen her brother. The last stroke of the Town Hall clock, however, had scarcely died away when she heard the patter of bare feet around the corner, and the next moment her brother, panting and breathless, stood before her.

"Oh, Nell!" he burst out, "I's just soft, I is. I's missed a hour in the time. I never did think I was sich a fool. But can't be helped now, nohow."

"I was afraid you'd got hurt, Benny; but I don't care now you're all right," said Nelly, looking proudly at the flushed face of her sturdy young brother.

"Me hurt? Oh, never fear! I knows how to take care of myself. But what luck, Nell?"

"Bad, Benny, very bad. Nobody wanted matches today."

For a moment Benny was silent, then he burst out, "By golly, Nell! what's us to do? You know what the guv'nor said when we came away this morning?"

"Ay," said Nelly. "But 'ave you 'ad bad luck too?"

"Horful, Nell – simply horful!"

And for a moment the children looked at each other in blank dismay. Just then a gentleman was seen crossing the street carrying a portmanteau.

"Here's a gent with a portmantle," whispered Benny to his sister. "I'll try my luck! Foller me, Nell, as quick as you can." And off he darted across the street.

"Carry yer bag, sir?" said he, stepping in front of the gentleman; and there was something very appealing in his tone as he spoke.

The gentleman looked kindly down into the two honest-looking eyes that flashed in the gaslight.

"What will you take the bag to the ferry for?" he inquired.

"For what you please to give," said Benny sturdily. "Times is bad at present, and little chaps like us is glad to 'ave what we catches."

"Oh, that's it, is it? But I'm afraid this bag is too heavy for you."

"Oh, never fear," said Benny, as he got hold of the portmanteau. "I'se 'mazing strong, and I ken carry this like winkin'." And he trotted down the street before the gentleman in a way that showed he was in earnest about the matter.

The gentleman looked after the little fellow with an amused smile, but volunteered no further remark.

Meanwhile little Nelly, who had become stiff and cramped with cold, followed at a little distance, taking care, however, that Benny did not get out of her sight. On reaching the bridge that led down to the landing-stage, Benny turned round, and, seeing his sister behind, shouted back, "Stay here, Nell, till I come back – I'll be no time sca'ce." And down the bridge he trotted, evidently glad that he was so near laying down his burden.

"Woodside boat, sir?" said he, turning round to the gentleman.

"Yes, my lad."

"Here we is, then, jist in time." And down the gangway he went at a sharp trot, and into the saloon, letting the bag down on one of the seats with a thump. "There you be, sir. Couldn't a-been sarved quicker by a bigger chap."

"All right, my little fellow," and he held out his hand.

Benny's eyes gleamed as he caught sight of something white between the gentleman's finger and thumb.

"Be jabbers! it's a thrip'ny," was his mental soliloquy, as he eagerly clutched the coin; and bowing his thanks as politely as he knew how, he dashed up the gangway with the fleetness of the wind, muttering to himself, "Shouldn't wonder if't was a fo'penny, arter all."

Standing under a lamp, he took the coin out of his mouth and looked at it. "Oh, glory!" he ejaculated; "if 't ain't haaf a bob. Murder and turf! this are a catch!" And he turned two somersaults on the stage by way of expressing his delight, unfortunately, however, planting his foot in his second revolution in the stomach of a young gentleman who was hurrying down to catch the boat.

The gentleman soon recovered his sudden loss of wind, though the dirty footprint on his immaculate coat was not so easily removed.

"Beg pardon," said Benny, in a fright, and hurried away just in time to escape a vigorous kick aimed at him by the infuriated young gentleman. "My stars and stockings!" he soliloquised, as he hurried up the bridge to join his sister. "If he 'ad a-catched me, I'd a-got a wolloping, an' no mistake. "Hello, Nell! what's a matter?" he said, as he saw great tears on the cheeks of his little crouching sister.

"I'se so cold, Benny – oh, so very cold!" sobbed the little girl.

"Never mind, Nelly, I'll soon get yer warmed up. Look here, I'se got haaf a bob, and a good warming into the bargain. Now for a roast tater, my gal, and you'll feel as right as ninepence."

And, taking his sister by the hand, they hurried away at a quick trot, lessening their pace only when they were quite out of breath, and Nelly declared she was quite warm.

"Here's the tater man," said Benny; "now for't, my gal. Pennorth o' taters – hot, plaise, an' a good sprinkle o' salt," said Benny, with quite an air of importance.

"All right, my young gent, 'ere you are," and the man put three moderate-sized potatoes into Benny's outstretched palms.

"Now for old Joe's fire, Nell, where the roads is a-mending" and once more they hurried away at the same quick trot.

In the next street they caught sight of the glowing grate of Joe Wrag, the night watchman, and of Joe himself, sitting in the doorway of his little wooden hut.

"You ax him, Nell," whispered Benny; "he winna say no to you."

"May we eat our taters by your fire, Joe?" said the plaintive voice of little Nelly, as she placed her tiny hand on the fence, on which a red light was burning.

"What dost 'a say, little woman?" said Joe, in a rough though not unkindly voice.

"May we eat our taters by your fire, please – Benny an' me?"

"Ay, ay, my little 'arties. Come along, I'll make room for 'e here;" and honest old Joe moved aside to make room for the little waifs who sought shelter from the biting cold.

"By golly, Nell!" said Benny, as he felt the grateful warmth of the fire, and dug his teeth into the potato; "ain't this sumpshus?"

"Ay, Benny," was all the child's answer, as she greedily devoured the two potatoes that Benny had insisted was her share.

Then there was silence between them for a while, and Joe went out and heaped more fuel on the grate, while Nelly kept her eyes steadily fixed on the fire. What did the child see as she gazed into its glowing depths? For ever and anon a sweet smile played around the corners of her mouth,

9

and spread over her pale thoughtful face, lighting it up with a wonderful beauty, and smoothing out the lines of care that at other times were only too visible.

Meanwhile, Benny was busily engaged counting his money. Fourpence he laid aside for the purpose of purchasing stock for the morrow's sale, a penny he had spent in potatoes, and still he had threepence to the good, besides the sixpence the gentleman gave him, which was clear profit. The sixpence was evidently a great prize to him, for he looked at it long and earnestly.

"Wish I could keep it for mysel'," he muttered; "but it's no go – the guv'nor will 'ave to 'ave it. But the coppers I'll keep 'ginst bad times. Here, Nell," he said, nudging his sister, "you keep these 'ere coppers; and then if the guv'nor axes me if I has any more, I can tell him no."

"All right, Benny." And again the great round eyes sought the glowing grate, and the sweet smile played over her face once more.

"What are 'e looking at, Nell?" said Benny, after a pause. "You look as 'appy as a dead duck in a saucepan."

"Oh, Benny, I see such beautiful pictures in the fire. Don't you 'members on fine days how we looks across the river, and sees the great hills 'way behind Birkenhead, such miles an' miles away?"

"Ay, I 'members. I'll take 'e across the river some day, Nell, when I'se richer."

"Will 'e, Benny? I shall be so glad. But I sees great hills in the fire, an' trees, an' pools, an' little rivers, an' oh! such lots of purty things."

"Queer!" said Benny. "I don't see nowt o' sort."

Then there was silence again, and Joe – who had been to see that the lamps at each end of the torn-up streets were all right – came up.

"How are 'e now, my 'arties? Are 'e warmer'n you was?"

"Ay, Joe, we's nice now," said Nelly; "an' we's much 'bliged to you for lettin' us come."

"Oh, ye're welcome. But ain't it time you was to home?"

"What's o'clock?" said Benny.

"Seven, all to a minit or so."

"Ay, then we must be off," said the children in chorus; and wishing Joe good night, they darted off into the wet, cold street, and disappeared in the gloom.

"Purty little hangel!" said Joe, as he stood looking up the street long after they had disappeared. "I wonder what will become o' her when she grows up?"

CHAPTER II

Addler's Hall

The whole court
Went boiling, bubbling up from all the doors
And windows, with a hideous wail of laughs
And roar of oaths, and blows, perhaps ... I passed
Too quickly for distinguishing, ... and pushed
A little side door hanging on a hinge,
And plunged into the dark.

Elizabeth Barrett Browning

ON the western side of Scotland Road – that is to say, between it and the Docks – there is a regular network of streets, inhabited mostly by the lowest class of the Liverpool poor. And those who have occasion to penetrate their dark and filthy recesses are generally thankful when they find themselves safe out again.

In the winter those streets and courts are kept comparatively clean by the heavy rains; but in the summer the air fairly reeks with the stench of decayed fish, rotting vegetables, and every other conceivable kind of filth.

The children, that seem to fairly swarm in this neighbourhood, are nearly all of a pale, sallow complexion, and of stunted growth. Shoes and stockings and underclothing are luxuries that they never know, and one good meal a day is almost more than they dare hope for.

Cuffs and kicks they reckon upon every day of their lives; and in this they are rarely disappointed, and a lad who by dodging or cunning can escape this daily discipline is looked upon by the others as "'mazin' cute".

To occupy two rooms is a luxury that only comparatively few families indulge in. Why should they pay rent for two rooms when one will answer the purpose? "We know a trick worth two o' that," is their boast. And so year by year they bid defiance to all law and authority.

The police rarely, if ever, venture into this neighbourhood alone, or if one should be foolish enough to do so, he has generally to pay dearly for his indiscretion. House agents and policemen are objects of special aversion.

A friend of ours, some years ago, came into considerable property in this neighbourhood, and employed a young man who was new to the work to collect the rents for him. On entering the first house the agent was confronted by a big, villainous-looking man, who demanded in a surly tone what he wanted.

"I am come for the rent," said the agent.

"Oh, you have, have you?" was the reply.

"Yes."

"Ah! Did anybody see you come in?"

"No."

And instantly seizing a huge poker and waving it in the air, he shouted to the affrighted agent, with a terrible oath, "Then I'll take care nobody ever sees you go out."

This had the desired effect, and the terrified agent escaped for his life. At the next house at which he called he was received very blandly.

"So you have come for the rint, have you?"

"Yes, that is my business."

"Ah, yes, indeed, very proper. Could you change a five

pun' note, now?"

"Oh, yes."

"That will do." Then raising his voice to a loud pitch, he shouted, "Mike, come down here; there's a chap that 'as five pun' in his pocket; let's collar him – quick!"

And a second time the affrighted agent fled, and gave up the situation at once, vowing he would never enter any of those streets again while he lived.

It was to this neighbourhood that Benny Bates and his sister wended their way, after leaving old Joe and his warm fire. Whether the lamplighter had neglected his duty, or whether some of the inhabitants, "loving darkness rather than light," had shut off the gas, is not certain; but anyhow Bowker's Row and several of the adjacent courts were in total darkness.

This, however, seemed no matter of surprise to Benny and little Nell, who wended their way without difficulty along the rough, ill-paved street. At length they turned up a narrow court, darker and dirtier even than Bowker's Row, which went by the name of 'Addler's Hall'. About half-way up this court they paused for a moment and listened; then, cautiously pushing open a door, they entered the only home they had ever known.

Much to their relief, they found the house empty. A lump of coal was smouldering in the grate, which Benny at once broke up, and soon a ruddy glare from the fire lighted up the dismal room.

The furniture consisted of a three-legged round table, a chair minus a leg, and a three-legged stool. On the window-sill there was a glass bottle with a candle stuck in the neck, and under the stairs there was a heap of rags and shavings, on which Benny and his sister slept. A frying-pan was suspended against the wall near the fireplace, and several cracked cups and saucers, together with a quart mug, stood on the table. The only other article of furniture was a small cupboard in a corner of the room close up to the ceiling, placed there, no doubt, to be out of the way of the children.

Drawing the chair and the stool close up to the fire, Benny and his sister waited the return of their parents.

Outside, the wind moaned and wailed, and whistled through the keyhole and the chinks in the door, and rattled the paper and rags with which the holes in the window were stopped. And as the children listened they shivered, and drew closer together, and nearer the fire.

"By golly!" said Benny, "this 'ouse is like a hair-balloon. I wish as how we could keep the wind out."

"You can't do that, Benny; it creeps in everywheres."

"Are 'e cold, Nell?"

"No, not very; but I's very hungry."

Just then an uncertain step was heard in the court outside, and the next moment their stepmother staggered into the room.

"Now, out of the way, you brats," was her greeting, "while I cooks your father's supper."

And without a word they got out of her way as quickly as possible, for they saw at a glance she was not in the best of humours. They were pleased to see, however, that she had brought with her a loaf of bread, some butter, and several red herrings, and so they were hopeful that for once they would get a good supper.

The supper was not quite ready when their father came in, flushed and excited.

"Where's the brats?" was his first angry exclamation, glancing round the room.

"There," said his wife, pointing under the stairs, where the children were crouched.

"Come out here, you young vermin; quick! do you hear?"

And the frightened children came out and stood before him.

"Have you brought me that sixpence that I told yer? For, if you ain't," said he, scowling at Benny, "I'll loosen yer hide for yer in double-quick time."

"Ay," said the little fellow, producing the sixpence, "ere it are."

"Is that all you've got?"

Benny shot a quick glance at his sister before replying, which, however, did not escape his father's eye.

"Ay," he said, stoutly; "I ain't got no more."

"You lie, you villain!" roared the father; "fork it out this moment."

"I tell yer I ain't got none," said Benny. Nelly was about to speak here, but a glance from her brother silenced her.

"Will you fork it out?" said the father again. "No," was the reply.

In a moment Dick Bates had taken the leather strap from his waist, and without mercy rained blow after blow upon the head and shoulders of his child.

At first Benny bore the blows without shrinking and without uttering a cry; but this only the more aggravated the inhuman father, and faster and more furious fell the blows, till the little fellow shrieked with pain and begged for mercy. But there was no mercy in the father's heart, and still the blows fell, till little Nelly, unable longer to bear it, rushed in between her father and brother, saying, "You shall not beat Benny so."

"Oh, you want it too, do you?" roared he. "Then take that, and that, and that."

"Father," said Benny, "will you strike Nell?"

The question for a moment seemed to stagger him, and

16

he looked down upon the pleading face of his suffering child, and into those great round eyes that were full of pain and tears, and the hand that was raised to strike fell powerless to his side, and with a groan he turned away.

What was there in the face of his little daughter that touched this cruel, besotted man? We cannot tell. Perhaps he caught a glimpse in that sweet face of his early love.

It is said that he loved his first wife dearly, and that while she lived he was tolerably steady, and was never unkind to her. He even went with her to the house of prayer, and listened to her while she read the Bible aloud during winter evenings. These were happy days, but when she died all this was changed; he tried to forget his trouble in drink, and in the companionship of the lowest and most degraded men and women.

Then he married again, a coarse drunken woman, who had ever since led him a wretched life; and every year he had become more drunken and vicious.

If he yet loved anything in the world, it was his "little Nell," as he always called her. She was wonderfully like her mother, the neighbours said, and that was doubtless the reason why Dick Bates continued to love her when all love for everything else had died out of his heart.

He had never treated her before as he had treated her tonight; it was a new experience to the child, and for long after she lay on her heap of shavings with dry eyes and hot cheeks, staring into vacancy.

But when the last spark of fire had died out, and her father and stepmother were asleep in the room above, turning to her brother, who was still awake, she said, "Put your arm about me, Benny, will yer?"

And Benny put his arm around his little sister, and pressed her face to his bosom. And then the fountain of the child's tears was broken up, and she wept as though her heart would break, and great sobs shook her little frame, and broke the silence of the night.

Benny silently kissed away the tears, and tried to comfort the little breaking heart. After a while she grew calm, and Benny grew resolute.

"I's not going to stand this no longer," he said.

"What will you do, Benny?"

"Do? Well, I dunno, yet; but I's bound to do some'at, an' I will too."

After a while he spoke again. "I say, Nell, ain't yer hungry? For I is. I believe I could eat a gravestun."

"I was hungry afore father beat me, but I doesna feel it now," was the reply.

"Well, I seen where mother put the bread an' butter, and if I dunna fork the lot, I's not Ben Bates."

"But how will yer get to it, Benny?"

"Aisy 'nough, on'y you must 'elp me."

So without much noise they moved the table into the corner of the room underneath the cupboard, and placing the chair on the top of the table, Benny mounted the top, and was able to reach the cupboard without difficulty.

A fair share of the loaf remained, and "heaps of butter," Benny said.

"Now, Nell," said he, "we'll 'ave a feast."

And a feast they did have, according to Benny's thinking, for very little of either loaf or butter remained when they had finished their repast.

"What will mother say when she finds out?" said Nelly, when they had again lain down.

"We must be off afore she wakes, Nell, and never come back no more."

"Dost 'a mean it, Benny?"

"Ay do I. We mun take all our traps wi' us i' t' morning."

"Where shall us go?"

"Never fear, we'll find a shop somewheres, an' anywheres is better nor this."

"Ay, that's so."

"Now, Nell, we mun sleep a bit, 'cause as how we'll 'ave to be stirring airly."

And soon the brother and sister were fast asleep, locked in each other's arms.

CHAPTER III

Roughing It

Ne'er saw I, never felt a calm so deep!
The river glideth at his own sweet will:
Dear God, the very houses seem asleep;
And all that mighty heart is lying still.

Wordsworth

NEXT morning Benny was stirring early, and when the first faint rays of the coming day peeped through the dust-begrimed and patched-up window, they saw the little fellow busily engaged in gathering together what things he and Nelly possessed previous to their final departure from home.

Nelly still slept on, and several times the brother paused and looked fondly down upon the fair face of the sleeping child. She looked very beautiful, Benny thought, as she lay sleeping there, with a pink spot glowing on either cheek, and the long flaxen hair thrown carelessly back from the pale forehead. Once or twice she murmured in her sleep, and the same happy smile spread over her face that he had noticed the evening before when she sat gazing into Joe Wrag's fire.

"I wonder what she's a-dreaming' on?" he murmured to himself. "Perhaps she sees the hills and flowers and trees agin."

Then he set to work again turning over a heap of rubbish

that had been pushed as far back as possible under the stairs. At length a joyful exclamation burst from his lips as he came upon a small heap of potatoes.

"Here's a fortin', an' no mistake; Nell and I'll be able to walk off the lot."

And he brought them out into the room, and wrapped them up in an old handkerchief that his stepmother used to tie round her head when she went out. There were scarcely twenty potatoes altogether, but to Benny they seemed almost an inexhaustible supply.

This being done, he sat down beside his sleeping sister and waited until he should hear any movement in the room above. Gradually the cold grey light of the morning stole into the room, revealing all its squalor and dinginess, and Benny felt that he and Nelly would have to make their escape soon, or else they might be prevented. He felt very loth to awake his sister, she slept so sweetly, and he did not know where they might find a shelter when darkness covered the earth again. But there was no help for it. His father might awake any moment, and the neighbours would soon be stirring in the court and in Bowker's Row. So bending over her, he pressed his lips upon her brow: still she moved not.

"Nelly," he whispered, "it's time to be movin'."

Slowly the great round eyes opened, and looked languidly up into his face.

"Come, stir your pegs, Nell, or we'll be too late."

"Oh, ay," she said, as the recollections of the previous evening came back to her. "We 'as to be off today, ain't we?"

"Ay, my gal, we's goin' on our own 'ook now, so look alive."

"Does yer think we's doin' right, Benny?"

"'Course we is, Nell; I'll take care o' you, never fear."

Thus reassured, she followed Benny silently out of the house and into Bowker's Row; then seeing that no one was about, they set off at a quick trot in the direction from whence they had come the previous night.

Nelly had the utmost confidence in Benny's sagacity, and though she had doubted for a moment whether they were doing the wisest thing in the course they were taking, yet she had little doubt that her brother would be equal to every emergency, and that he would find her a home of some sort. And the child had a vague, undefined feeling that they could not be worse off, whatever might happen. To see her Benny punished as she had so frequently done of late was "pain and grief" to her: not only had he suffered the pinchings of cold and hunger during the day, but he had been compelled to bring home a certain amount every night, or else take the consequences of her father's senseless anger.

And as the child thought of these things she could not wonder that Benny had resolved to run away and seek a home somewhere else. But what of herself? She had on the whole been much better treated, and she thought perhaps her father did not well know what he was doing last night, as he was in drink. Ought she, then, to run away?

"Ay, but I cannot leave Benny," was her mental response; and having settled that question, she seemed perfectly satisfied to share the fortunes of her brother, whatever they might be, and help him as best she could to fight the battle of life.

As for Benny, he had no qualms of conscience about the matter. He had never heard the command, "Honour thy father and thy mother," and even if he had, it would not have troubled him on the present occasion. He had a feeling that he had been wronged, cruelly wronged, and that he ought not to stand it any longer. Once the question had crossed his mind, "Had he any right to take those potatoes?" But he answered the question to himself by saying, "Ain't I brought home a haaf a bob every night for th' week, an' then bin kept without supper? By jabbers, I's paid for those taters, and I'll eat 'em." Moreover, his notions of right and wrong were of the vaguest character. He had some dim recollection of his mother, and how she used to tell him it was wrong to steal, and to tell lies, and to cheat. But the more he tried to recall it, the vaguer the recollection became. Yet sometimes when he was tempted to steal, and would look around to see that no one was watching him, a voice within him would whisper, "Don't, Benny, it is wrong to steal," and he would turn away with a sigh, feeling that there was something in that voice that he dared not disobey.

In after years he held firmly to the belief that his own mother was permitted to be the guardian angel of his childhood, and that it was she who whispered to him when he was tempted to do wrong. He has also been heard to say, that though he regarded it as very wrong for children, under ordinary circumstances, to leave their home without their parents' consent, yet in his case he thought his action perfectly justifiable.

But we must leave this question, with the hope that none of the children who read this story may lie driven by cruelty and wrong to a similar course of action, and must follow the little waifs as they threaded their way through the dingy streets that cold December morning. Their object was to reach Joe Wrag's fire before his watch ended, and in this they were successful. Joe was standing before his hut, rubbing his hands over the still glowing grate, though Benny noticed that the fire was burning low.

"We's brought some taters from home, may we cook 'em

23

on yer fire, Joe?" said Benny, putting on as bold a face as he could. Joe looked at the children for a moment without speaking.

"Please do, Joe, like a good man," chimed in Nelly's plaintive voice.

"Come along with yer, then. But how are 'e out so airly?"

"Lots o' bisness on hand," was Benny's prompt reply.

"There's some'at up wi' you youngsters, I reckon. But yer not goin' to eat all these taters at once, are yer?"

"Oh, no!" said Benny, "we on'y want two apiece, and we want you to keep the rest till we comes agin."

"Very likely story," said Joe, gruffly. "Where's yer bin stealin' 'em from?"

"Oh, nowheres, Joe," said Nelly. "We bringed 'em from home, we did, for sure."

"Well, ain't that a-stealin' on 'em?"

"No!" said Benny, stoutly. "I's tooked 'em home a haaf a bob every night for t' week, and they b'longs to me."

Joe shook his head dubiously, as if not certain of the soundness of Benny's logic, but made no further reply. He, however, gave his aid to the children in cooking their potatoes, which were soon done to a nicety, and even gave them a piece of bread, the remains of his own morning's repast. Thus fortified, the children were soon ready for the duties of the day.

Their first business was to go into Park Lane and get in a stock of matches for the day's sale; this done, they separated and went their different ways, agreeing to meet in the shadow of St. George's Church at twelve o'clock, and at four to report progress.

Nelly's stand was near the junction of Lord Street, Church Street, Paradise Street, and Whitechapel, going occasionally as far as the Sailors' Home. Benny, on the other hand, waited about near the landing-stage, selling his matches if he could, but at the same time looking out for an opportunity of carrying some gentleman's bag.

But today Benny had another object in view, and that was to discover, if possible, some place where he and his sister might sleep when night came on. He knew of a place where, for the payment of a penny each, they might sleep in a cellar on some dirty straw amongst a lot of rough boys. But somehow Benny shrank from introducing his sister to such company as there assembled night after night. He must find some place where they could be alone, if possible, though he felt that that would be no easy matter.

The day was beautifully fine, with a clear frosty sky, and both Benny and his sister carried on a brisk sale in fusees, and when they met at noon they were in high spirits over the proceeds of the day. Still Benny had found no place as yet where to spend the night.

During the afternoon, however, his attention was directed to some sailors who were caulking a boat not far from the George's Dock. The boat he noticed was turned bottom upward, and that it had one end stove in; evidently it had had rough handling somewhere. And besides this, Benny noticed that there was a large quantity of hemp and tow on which the sailors were kneeling while at their work. Several times during the afternoon he took a look at the sailors, and when at length he saw them lift up the boat and push the tow underneath, his mind was made up.

"Stunnin'!" he ejaculated; "I b'lieve we is in luck's way today. Couldna have bin better if it were a-made for us."

Punctually at four o'clock the children were at their trysting-place. They were both in high spirits, for their profits were larger than they had been for many a day past. Benny especially was in high glee, for he had the prospect of a comfortable lodging-place for the night, without any fear of his father's fury, and was consequently eager to communicate his discovery to Nelly.

"Golly, Nell," was his greeting, using his favourite expression, "it's a heap too cold to stick in one place. Let's off into Park Lane, and git a feed; we can 'ford it tonight."

And off they started, hand in hand. The place to which they directed their steps was not the most select, the character of the customers being of no consequence, so long as the money was forthcoming. This fact was well known to Benny, so he entered, leading his sister by the hand, without any trepidation. It was a long narrow room in which they found themselves, with several small tables placed at regular intervals down the sides. A bright fire was burning in the farther end of the room, near which Benny took his seat, requesting that "two penny loaves might be brought, and a pennorth of cheese."

They remained as long as they felt they dared, then again sought the wintry streets. But the keen frosty air made them long for shelter, and once more they sought the glowing grate of honest Joe Wrag. The old man seemed pleased to see them, and made room for them in his hut, though he said little. Oh, how the fire glowed and crackled in the keen frosty air, revealing to little Nelly Bates scenes of wondrous beauty! And as Joe watched her face glowing in the firelight, he muttered to himself, "Purty little hangel; I hopes she'll grow up good, or … or die – ay, or die!"

It was after eight o'clock when they left Joe's warm hut, for Nelly had pleaded so hard to stay that he could not deny her request. She seemed to be twining herself around the old man's heart in a wonderful manner, and but for his fury of a wife he would have taken her to his own home when it became known to him that the children were homeless.

It did not take them long to reach the boat; and having satisfied themselves that they were not noticed, they crept underneath in a "jiffey," as Benny would have expressed it.

"Brimstone and treacle!" said Benny, as he put his hand on the large heap of tow; "ain't this sumpshus? We'll be as snug as Jonar 'ere."

"Ay, Benny, this is fine."

"Let's shut out all the daylight fust, Nell, an' then the cold won't git in."

Thanks to the abundance of tow this was not difficult, and soon the children were cuddled in each other's arms, feeling warmer than they had felt for many a night past. It was a long time, however, before they could get to sleep. To Nelly especially was it strange. And thoughts too deep for them to express kept crowding into their minds, keeping them wide awake.

At length, however, a feeling of drowsiness began to creep over them, and they were just dropping off to sleep when they were startled by a footstep near them, and a hoarse voice muttering, as if in anguish, "O Death, what dost thou mean?"

For a moment, the children clutched each other in terror; then they heard the footsteps dying away in the distance, and their confidence returned again. "Who could it be?" said Nelly.

"A bobby, I'specks," said Benny; "but he ain't catched us, so we's safe 'nough now."

For a while after they lay listening, but no other footsteps disturbed them, and soon balmy sleep stole over them, sealing their eyelids, and giving rest to their weary little heads and hearts.

CHAPTER IV

A Friend in Need

Friendship, peculiar boon of heaven,
The noble mind's delight and pride;
To men and angels only given,
To all the lower world denied.

Samuel Johnson

THE experiences of Benny and his sister during the next day were but a repetition of what we recorded in the last chapter; but during the second night they found the shelter of the boat but a poor substitute for a home, and in the morning they were stiff and cramped through lying so long in one position; and when they paid Joe Wrag their third morning visit, the old man noticed that all was not right with them. Nelly especially was gloomy and depressed.

Joe Wrag was generally a silent man, and not given to asking many questions; but when he saw great tears in Nelly's round eyes as she sat gazing into the fire, he felt that he must know what was troubling the child, and help her if he could. He had also a dim suspicion that they had not been to their home of late, and he wondered where they could have spent their nights; and, like Benny, he dreaded the idea of little Nelly congregating with young thieves and vagabonds, and felt he would rather a thousand times the child should die than that she should grow up to be a wicked woman. So after reflecting for some time, and wondering how he should best get at the truth, he burst out suddenly with the question, "When were ye last home, eh?"

For a moment there was silence, and Benny looked at his sister as much as to say, "That's a poser; we're in for it now."

"Come, now," said Joe, seeing their hesitation, "let's 'ave nowt but truth; out wi' it, an' it will be best in the end."

"You tell 'im, Nell," said Benny, "'cause he'll b'lieve you."

So Nelly, in her sweet pleading voice, told him all the story of Benny's wrong, and of her father's cruelty, and how even she herself had not escaped his anger.

"And did he beat you, my purty?" said Joe, clenching his fist tightly at the same time.

"Ay, Joe; but I dunna think he know'd what he were a-doin'."

For a few moments the old man's face worked as if in pain. Then he muttered to himself, "Some'at must be done, an' no mistake; but what? Eh, what?" Then he looked at the children again.

"Don't yer think you'd better go home again tonight?" he said; and he watched eagerly for the effect of his question. Nelly was the first to speak.

"Oh, no," she said; "we should get it worse nor ever. Dad would a'most kill Benny." And the tears welled up into her eyes again.

"I's not goin' to risk it," said Benny, stoutly. "I's 'ad hidin's enough to last me a lifetime."

"Ay, ay," said Joe. "I wonder, now ..." And he looked reflectively into the fire.

"What are 'e a-wonderin' on?" queried Benny.

But Joe was silent. He had evidently got hold of some idea which he was trying to work out. At length he looked up and said, "Now, away with yer, an' come here again this

29

ev'ning at six o'clock. D' ye hear?"

"Ay, ay," was the response; and away they bounded, leaving Joe alone to his meditations.

Joe remained some time after they were gone in one position, scratching his head most vigorously, and would doubtless have remained much longer had he not been disturbed by the men who had come to their work, and who set him at liberty from his watch until darkness should again come down upon the earth. Joe walked leisurely to his home as if burdened with some great thought, ate his morning meal in silence, and then went to bed, and lay tossing fully two hours ere he could find a wink of sleep.

Joe Wrag had been for many years a complete enigma to a number of well-meaning people, who had become much interested in this silent and thoughtful man, and were anxious to know more about him than he cared to reveal. Several 'town missionaries' had tried to make something out of him, but had utterly failed. He had never been known to enter a house of prayer, and whether in the matter of religious knowledge and belief he was a heathen or a Christian was an open question; and yet, notwithstanding this, he lived a life that in many respects was worthy of the imitation of many who made greater professions.

Indeed, to be strictly accurate, Joe Wrag never made any profession whatever of any kind, and yet he was as honest as the day, and as true as steel. Honest, not because 'honesty was the best policy'. Nay, policy never entered into his thoughts; but he was honest because he could not be otherwise. His soul was honest; and as for lying, he loathed it as he would loathe a viper. Nothing could tempt him to be untruthful. In fact, he recoiled as if by instinct from everything mean and deceitful. What teaching he had received, or what influences had surrounded him during his early life, we have never been able to gather. He kept himself mostly to himself, and was silent about the past. Year by year he moved along the even tenor of his way, ever ready to do a kindly deed when opportunity presented itself; but never thrusting himself where he felt he might not be wanted. He had a perfect horror of appearing to be better than he really was; and it was thought that that was his chief reason why he never made any profession of religion.

About three o'clock Joe got up, and after partaking of a substantial meal, wended his way to the neighbourhood of Copperas Hill. After turning several sharp corners, he found himself in a small court containing about half a dozen houses. Before one of the doors he paused for a moment, then raised his stick, and gave a sharp rat-tat-tat. The door was instantly opened by a woman who had evidently reached her threescore years and ten. Yet she appeared hale and strong for her age, and though poorly, was yet tidily attired.

"Well, ye are a stranger," was her greeting. "I'm verra glad to see 'e, though."

"An' I'm glad to see you, Betty."

"Well, come tha in. What's i' tha wind?"

"Nowt much, Betty; but what thar is consarns you as much as me."

Well, out wi' it, Joe," said Betty, as soon as Joe had seated himself. "No trouble, I 'ope?"

"No, not that I knows on; but could 'e make room 'ere for a couple o' lodgers – little 'uns, mind you – children on'y 'bout so high?" holding out his hand.

"Well, what an idear, to be sure! What are ye a-dreamin' on?"

"Your old man," said Joe solemnly, "was my mate for mony a year, an' a good man he wur; an' if from that fur-off country he can see what's doin' 'ere, he'd be mightily

31

pleased for 'e to do, Betty, what I'm a-axin' o' yer.'

"But I dunno that I quite understand," said Betty; "explain your meanin' a bit more."

And Joe, in a solemn voice, told the story of little Nell and her brother Benny. "It mebbe, Betty," he said, "they're the Lord's little 'uns. I'm none o' the Lord's mysel'. I've tried to find 'im; but He winna be found o' me. I'm none o' the elect. I've settled that for more'n twenty year now. But if these bairns are the Lord's, we mustna turn 'em away."

"All bairns are the Lord's," said Betty; but Joe only shook his head, and sat gazing into the fire.

Before he left, however, it was settled that a bed should be made for the children in the corner under the stairs, which would be near the fire also. For this they were to pay a penny per night.

"We mustna make paupers o' them, you know, Betty," was Joe's remark.

It was also agreed that she should do what washing and mending the children's clothes needed, for which they were to pay also, if they could afford it. "If not," said Joe, "I'll make it square wi' you, Betty."

Punctually, at six o'clock, the children put in an appearance at Joe's hut. They had had but poor luck during the day, and Benny did not feel nearly so courageous as he had felt two days before. The prospect of sleeping night after night underneath a boat was not so inviting as he had imagined it would be; besides, there was the fear that their hiding-place might be discovered, and that even this poor shelter might be taken away from them at any time.

He did not confide his fears to Nelly; he felt that it would be cruel to do so; and she – whatever she may have felt – never uttered a single word of complaint. She knew that 'her Benny' had enough to bear, and she would not add to his burden.

Benny had been very much puzzled at Joe Wrag's manner in the morning, and had wondered much during the day "what he 'ad been a-turnin' over in his noddle". He was desperately afraid that Joe would try to persuade him and Nelly to return to their home, or even insist upon their doing so; and rather than do that, he felt that he would lose Joe's friendship and warm fireside into the bargain.

Joe was looking very abstractedly into the grate when they came up to the fence, and for a moment they watched his rugged face with the firelight playing upon it. But Benny, who could read his father's face pretty cleverly, declared to himself that "he could make nowt out o' Joe's".

As usual, Joe made room for Benny in his little hut; but tonight he took little Nelly very tenderly on his knee, and stroked her long flaxen hair with his hard rough hand, muttering to himself the while, "Purty little hangel; I reckon she's one o' the Lord's elect."

Benny wondered for a long time when Joe was going to say something that he could understand; but somehow tonight he did not like to disturb him by asking questions. Nelly, on the contrary, was far away again from the cold and dingy streets, and the ceaseless roar of the busy town, and was wandering in imagination through sunny meadows where the turf was soft and the grass was green. She fancied she heard the music of purling streams, and the songs of happy birds in the leafy trees that waved their branches over her. The air was fragrant with the scent of flowers that she had heard of, but never seen, and weariness and cold she felt no more.

The voice of Joe banished the beautiful vision from the glowing grate, and the child wondered if ever it would become a reality – if ever she would dwell amid such scenes in a life that had no ending.

"I've some'at to say to 'e, my dears," was Joe's first exclamation; and the children looked up into his face, and wondered what was coming next. "I've found a home for 'e, and a reet good 'un, an' ye'r to go tonight."

"Oh, scissors!" shouted Benny; and he ran into the street, and had turned two somersaults ere he knew what he was doing; then stood on his head for at least five seconds by way of cooling off, and what other performances he might have gone through I cannot say, had not Joe called him into the hut.

Little Nelly said nothing; she only nestled closer to her benefactor, and Joe felt great scalding tears dropping upon his hand, and knew that her heart was too full for speech. Then he told them all about their new home, and what would be expected of them, and how he hoped they would be good and kind to the old woman, and always be honest and truthful, and then when they died they might go to the good place.

"Does folks go somewheres when they die?" said Benny, with a look of astonishment.

"Ay, Ben, that they do."

"Oh, beeswax and turpentine!" he ejaculated, "that are a go!"

But Nelly's face grew luminous, and her eyes fairly sparkled, as she faintly grasped the idea that perhaps her dreams might come true after all.

They had no difficulty in finding their way to Tempest Court, or in discovering the house of Betty Barker. The old woman gave them a rough though kindly welcome, and Benny was soon at his ease. Their bed in the warm corner under the stairs was, to use Benny's phrase, "simply sumshus"; and next morning when they appeared before Joe, it was with faces glowing with gladness and delight.

CHAPTER V

"Oh Death,
What Dost Thou Mean?"

To sleep! perchance to dream; – ay, there's the rub;
For in that sleep of death what dreams may come,
When we have shuffled off this mortal coil,
Must give us pause.

Hamlet

WE must now go back to the morning when Benny and his sister left their home, and pay one more visit to 'Addler's Hall'.

Dick Bates got up in the morning with a splitting headache, and, if the truth must be told, with an aching heart. His sleep had been disturbed by horrid dreams, the recollection of which haunted him still, and made him feel anything but comfortable. He had dreamt that he had been working near the docks, and in going close to the edge of one of them he saw his two children rise to the surface of the water clasped in each other's arms; and while he looked at them, they opened their glassy eyes and cast upon him one lingering, reproachful glance, then sank to the bottom again. Twice during the night had this dream been repeated, and when he awoke in the morning it was with a vague fear of impending evil. Dick Bates, like many other hardened and cruel men, was at heart a great coward, besides being very superstitious. He listened several times for any movement downstairs, but all was still; and this only increased his alarm, for he knew his children were in the habit of stirring early, and he saw by the light that the morning was far advanced.

We may judge, therefore, of his alarm when, on coming downstairs, he found the room empty, and he thought, with a terror in his heart that made the perspiration ooze from his forehead, that perhaps his children had been driven by his cruelty to put an end to their existence.

He tried to banish the thought as weak and childish, but he could not; his nerves were completely unstrung today, and he did not seem at all himself. When his wife came down he sent her into the neighbours' houses, and into Bowker's Row, to inquire if anyone had seen them. But everywhere the same answer was given: no one had either seen them or heard them. His wife characterised his fears as 'bosh', and declared, "He wur wuss nor any owd woman. The brats'll turn up agin tonight, never fear," she said; and Dick sincerely hoped in his heart that they would do so. He was too late to get any work that morning, so he spent most of the forenoon in the house, brooding over his fears. And while he sat there on the low stool with his face buried in his hands, memories of other and happier years crowded in upon his brain. His boyhood life in the country seemed to him now, as he looked back at it through a long vista of years, like a happy dream. And he was glad that his old father and mother were dead, and did not know how low he had fallen.

Then he thought of the morning when he had led his first young bride to church, and of the few short years of happiness that had followed. He remembered, too, the promise he had made her on her dying bed – that he would take care of the children, and meet her in heaven. Alas! how he had belied those solemn words! He had not cared for his children, he admitted to himself with shame; but, on the contrary, he had cruelly neglected them, had behaved towards them as the veriest brute. And now perhaps they were dead – driven to death by his cruelty.

Then other thoughts took possession of him. "If they're dead," he said, "they are better off: what is there to live for? Better for 'em to die now than to grow up to be like me and Sal."

Then he began to wonder what dying meant. "If I wur sartin," he said, "that there wur nowt arter death, I'd die too." And he got up and walked about the room; after a while he sat down again, and buried his face in his hands once more. "Mary used to say," he mused, "that bad people went to a bad place an' was tormented forever; but that if we was good, an' trusted in the Saviour, we should go to 'eaven an' be 'appy for ever. And poor owd father and mother used to say t' same. I remembers it very well! Ah me, I've nearly forgot all sense o' it, though."

And thus he mused hour after hour, heedless that his wife swore and raved that, "The brats had eat all the butter, and walked off wi' all the taters."

When, however, he was made to comprehend this fact, he became less concerned about his children, and a little before noon he started off in search of work. But all the afternoon he was gloomy and depressed, and instead of going to a public house, as was his wont when the day's work was done, he set off home, much to the surprise of his mates, who grew warm in a discussion as the evening advanced as to what "'ad a-comed over Dick Bates".

From seven to nine he sat in his own desolate home alone, for his wife was in no humour to keep him company, and every patter of feet in the court made him start and look eagerly towards the door, in the hope that he would see it open, and his children enter; but the door did not open, and his children never came.

"I wouldna a-minded so much," he said, "if I hadna a-wolloped poor little Nell," and he vowed with a terrible oath that he would "treat 'em better in t' future, if ever I 'ave the chance."

But when the clock in the steeple not far away struck nine, he started up, muttering to himself, "I canna stand this: I wonder what's comed to me? If 't bairns would come home, I reckon I'd be all right." But the bairns did not come, and he started out to get a glass, to help him to drown remorse.

His mates tried to rally him, but they had to confess that it was a 'no go' and when at eleven o'clock he left them at the corner of the street, and once more directed his steps towards Addler's Hall, they touched their foreheads significantly to each other, and whispered it as their opinion that Dick Bates was "a-goin' wrong in his noddle," and was "above a bit luny".

When he reached his home, he opened the door with a beating heart. All was silent, save the heavy breathing of his wife in the room above. He went to the dark corner where his children slept, and felt with his hands; but the bed, such as it was, was empty, and with a groan he turned away and hid his face in his hands. And again his past life came back to him more vividly than it had done for years.

"I mun go an' look for 'em," he said. "I shall see 'em floating in one o' the docks, as I did last night in my dream." And with a feeling of despair in his heart he wandered forth again into the now almost deserted streets.

As we have before stated, it was a clear frosty night; not a single cloud obscured the myriad stars that glittered in the deep vault of heaven. And as Dick Bates wandered under the light of the stars along the long line of docks, no one would have believed that this anxious-faced man was the brutal drunkard that only on the previous night punished his unoffending children without mercy.

Was it God that was working in his heart, bringing back to him the memories of other years, and awaking within him better thoughts? Who shall say it was not?

Still on he went, starting continually as he fancied he saw something white on the dark still water. "How nice it would be," he muttered, "to sleep for ever! to be free fra the worry an' trouble. But how could he know that death was endless sleep? Might it not be, as his Mary said it was, the beginning of a life that should never end? He was now near the boat under which his children lay. It was his footstep that startled them just as they were dropping off to sleep. It was his voice that muttered the words, "O Death! what dost thou mean?"

How near father and children had come to each other! but neither knew of the other's presence: then they drifted apart again, to meet no more on earth. There were only a few small vessels in the next dock, and all the lights were out.

"There they be, sure enough," said Dick, as something white, floating on the surface of the water, caught his eye, and he went close up to the edge of the dock, forgetful of the fact that the huge damp coping-stones had, by the action of the frost, become as slippery as glass. He had scarcely planted his foot on one of the huge stones when it slipped from beneath him; a piercing shriek rang out on the startled air, followed by a plunge, a gurgling cry, and the cold water closed over him.

A moment later, a pale agonised face gleamed up from the dark water, a hurried prayer floated up on the cold frosty air, "Saviour of my Mary, save me!" then the water closed over him again. Two other times, at longer intervals, Dick Bates' agonised and horror-stricken face appeared for a moment on the surface; then the ruffled waters grew smooth, hiding in their dark bosom the dead body of Richard Bates, whose soul had been so suddenly called to its account.

The next day the dead body was dragged to the surface, and conveyed to the dead-house, where it was claimed by his wife. An inquest and a funeral followed, of which Benny and little Nell never knew. And it was well, perhaps, they did not. The knowledge would have been pain to the little waifs, and they had already as much trouble as their little hearts knew how to bear.

CHAPTER VI

In Which Benny
Makes a Discovery

All unseen the Master walketh
By the toiling servant's side;
Comfortable words He speaketh,
While His hands uphold and guide.

Baynes

CHRISTMAS DAY this year came upon a Wednesday, and, during the two days preceding it, Benny did what he characterised as a "roaring bizness". There were so many people leaving and arriving by all the ferry-boats and at all the stations, that our hero was kept on the trot nearly all the time. His frank open face seemed to most people, who had a bag or a bundle to carry, a sufficient guarantee of his honesty, and they hoisted their bag upon the little fellow's shoulder without any fear that he would attempt to pry into its contents, or make off with it round some sharp corner.

For a time the 'match business' was turned over entirely to Nelly's management; and though the modest little girl never pushed her wares – she was too shy for that – yet Benny declared she did "stunnin'".

Many a gentleman, catching just a glimpse of the pale

sweet face as he hurried past, would turn to have another look at the child, and, without taking any of her fusees, would put a penny, and sometimes more, into the little thin hand. And Nelly would curtsy her thanks, unable to utter a word.

Benny declared that, "He liked Christmas-time 'mazin' well, and wondered why folks didn't have Christmas a sight oftener than once a year." How it was that coppers were so much more plentiful at this time of the year than at any other time was to him a mystery. Poor little fellow! the thought never seemed to enter into his small head that it might be that people's hearts were more open at this festive season than at some other times. However, Benny was not one that speculated long on such questions; he only wished that people were always as ready to have their bags carried, and always gave their pence as ungrudgingly.

Once or twice he felt a bit sad, and brushed away a hasty tear, when he saw boys no bigger than himself wrapped up in great warm overcoats, and beautiful little girls with fur-trimmed jackets and high-heeled dainty boots, clasped in the arms of their parents as soon as they stepped from the ferry, and then hurried away to a cab, or to a carriage in waiting – and then thought of his own cheerless life. "I specks they's mighty 'appy," he said reflectively, and then walked away to the other end of the stage, where he thought he saw the chance of employment.

On Christmas Eve Benny took his sister through St. John's Market, and highly delighted they were with what they saw. The thousands of geese, turkeys, and pheasants, the loads of vegetables, the heaps of oranges and apples, the pyramids of every other conceivable kind of fruit, the stalls of sweetmeats, the tons of toffee, and the crowds of well-dressed people all bent upon buying something, were sources of infinite pleasure to the children. There was only one drawback to their happiness, and that was they did not know how to lay out the sixpence they had brought with them to spend. If there had been less variety there would have been less difficulty; but, as it was, Benny felt as if he would never be able to decide what to buy. However, they agreed at last to lay out twopence in two slices of bread and ham, for they were both rather hungry; and then they speculated the other fourpence in apples, oranges, and toffee, and, on the whole, felt very well satisfied with the result of their outlay.

It was rather later than usual when they got home, but old Betty knew where they had gone, and, as it was Christmas Eve, she had got a bigger fire in than usual, and had also got them a cup of hot cocoa each, and some bun loaf to eat with it.

"By golly!" said Benny, as he munched the cake, "I do wish folks 'ud 'ave Christmas ev'ry week."

"You are a cur'us boy," said the old woman, looking up with a smile on her wrinkled face.

"Is I, granny? I specks it's in my blood, as the chap said o' his timber leg."

The old woman had told them on the first evening of their arrival, when they seemed at a loss what name to give her, to call her granny; and no name could have been more appropriate, or have come more readily to the children's lips.

"But could folks 'ave Christmas any oftener if they wished to?" asked little Nell.

"In course they could, Nell," burst out Benny. "You dunna seem to know what folks make Christmas for."

"An' I thinks as you dunno either, Benny."

"Don't I, though?" he said, putting on an air of importance. "It's made to give folks the chance of doing a lot o' feeding; didn't yer see all the gooses an' other nice things in the market that the folks is going to polish off to-morrow?"

"I dunna think it was made purpose for that. Wur it, now, granny?"

Thus appealed to, the old woman, who had listened with an amused smile on her face, answered, "No, my child. It's called Christmas 'cause it is the birthday of Christ."

"Who's He?" said Benny, looking up; and Nelly's eyes echoed the inquiry.

"Don't you know – ain't you never heerd?" said the old woman, in a tone of surprise.

"Nay," said Benny; "nothin' sense. Some o' the chaps says 'by Christ' as I says 'by golly'; but I never knowed He was somebody."

"Poor little dears! I didn't know as how you was so ignorant, or I should have told you before." And the old woman looked as if she did not know where or how to begin to tell the children the wonderful story, and for a considerable time remained silent. At length she said, "I'll read it to 'e out o' the Book; mebbe you'll understand it better that way nor any way else."

And taking down from her shelf her big and much-worn Bible, she opened it at the second of St. Matthew, and began to read in a tremulous voice, "Now when Jesus was born in Bethlehem of Judaea in the days of Herod the king, behold, there came wise men from the east to Jerusalem, saying, Where is He that is born King of the Jews? for we have seen His star in the east, and are come to worship Him."

And slowly the old woman read on until she reached the end of the chapter, while the children listened with wide-open and wondering eye. To Nelly, the words seemed to come like a revelation, responding to the deepest feeling of her nature, and awakening thoughts within her that were too big for utterance. Benny, however, on the contrary, could see nothing particularly interesting in the narrative itself.

But the art of reading was to him a mystery past all comprehension. How granny could see that story upon the page of her Bible was altogether beyond his grasp. At length, after scratching his head vigorously for some time, he burst out, "By jabers! I's got it at last! – Jimmy Jones squeeze me if I ain't! It's the specks that does it."

"Does what?" said Nelly.

"Why, the story bizness, to be sure. Let me look at the book through your specks, shall I, granny?"

"Ay, if you like, Benny." And the next minute he was looking at the Bible with granny's spectacles upon his nose, with a look of blank disappointment upon his face.

"Golly? I's sold!" was his exclamation. "But this are a poser, and no mistake."

"What's such a poser?" said granny.

"Why, how yer find the story in the book; for I can see nowt." And Benny looked as disappointed as if he had earned nothing for a week.

By much explaining, however, granny enabled him to comprehend in some vague way how the mystery was accomplished; and then arose within the heart of the child an unutterable longing to understand this mysterious art fully, and be able to read for himself – a longing that grew in intensity as evening after evening he tried, by granny's help, to master the alphabet. In fact, it became a passion with the lad, and many an hour in the weeks and months that followed he spent gazing at the placards on the walls, and in trying to explain to the other Arabs that gathered around him the meaning of the mysterious characters.

Benny was naturally a sharp lad, and hence, though his opportunities were few, his progress was by no means slow. Sometimes he startled Joe Wrag by spelling out a long word that he had carried in his head the whole of the day, and

45

asking its meaning. Long words had an especial fascination for him, and the way he brought them out in all sorts of connections was truly amusing.

Nelly manifested no desire to learn to read. If ever she thought about it, it was only to regard it as something infinitely beyond her capabilities; and she seemed content to remain as she was. But if she could get granny to read to her a chapter out of St. John's Gospel, she seemed to desire no higher pleasure. She would sit with a dreamy far-away look in her half-closed eyes, and the smiles that old Joe Wrag loved to see would come and go upon her face like patches of spring sunshine chasing each other across a plain. She never said very much, but perhaps she thought all the more. To honest Joe Wrag she seemed as if ripening for a fairer country, and for a purer and nobler life. Not that she ailed anything. True, she had a little hacking cough now and then, and when she lay asleep a pink spot would glow on either cheek; but nothing more than that.

"Speretual things," mused Joe Wrag one night, as he sat in the door of his hut looking into the fire, "are speretually discerned, an' I b'lieve that child 'as rale speretual discernment: she looks a mighty sight deeper than we thinks she do, that's my opinion. I should like to get howld o' all that passes through her purty little noddle, the little hangel – bless her! As for the boy, 'e's a little hammal. I reckon the passons would call him a materialist. I don't b'lieve 'e b'lieves nothing but what 'e sees. No speretual insight in 'im – not a bit. P'r'haps he's like me, don't belong to the elect. Ah, me! I wonder what the likes o' us was born for?"

And Joe went out, and heaped more fuel on the fire by way of diverting his thoughts from a subject that was always painful to him. But when he came back and sat down again, and the fire before him blazed up with fiercer glow, the thoughts returned, and would not be driven away.

"Bless her!" he said. "She sees in the fire only woods, an' meadows, an' mountains, an' streams; an' I only see the yawning caverns o' hell. An' to think I must burn in a fire a thousan' times bigger an' hotter than that for ever and ever without a single moment's ease; scorchin' on every side, standin' up or lyin' down, always burnin'! No water, no light, no mercy, no hope. And when a million million years are past, still burnin', an' no nearer the end than at the beginnin'. Oh, how shall I bear it – how shall I bear it?"

And big drops of perspiration oozed from his forehead and rolled down his face, testifying to the anguish of his soul.

"I canna understand it – I canna understand it," he went on. "All this pain and suffering for His glory. What kind o' glory can it be, to bring folks into the world doomed aforehand to eternal misery? to give 'em no chance o' repentance, an' then damn them for ever 'cause they don't repent! O Lord a mercy, excuse me, but I canna see no justice in it anywhere."

And once more Joe got up and began to pace up and down in front of the fire; but the thoughts would not leave him. "'Whom He did foreknow,'" he went on, "'them also He did predestinate.' Mighty queer, that a Father should love a part o' His fam'ly an' hate the rest. Create 'em only to burn 'em for ever an' ever! An' what's the use o' the burning'? That bangs me complete. If 't was to burn away the dross an' leave the metal, I could understand it. I think sometimes there's jist a bit o' the right stuff in me; an' if hell would burn up the bad an' leave the good, an' give it a chance of some'at better, there 'ud be more justice in it, seems to me. But what am I a-saying? It shows as how I'm none o' the elect, to be talking to myself in this way. What a wicked old sinner I be!"

47

And once more Joe sat down with a jerk, as if he meant to say, "I'm not going to be bothered with such thoughts any more tonight." But alas! he found that thoughts would come whether he would or no.

"P'r'haps," he said, "we don't know nowt about it, none o' us. Mebbe God is more marcyfuller than we think. An' I'm sadly banged about that 'makin' an end o' sin;' I don't see as how He can make an end o' sin without making an end o' the sinner; an' whiles there is millions sich as me in hell, there'll be no end to neither on 'em. I'm sadly out in my reck'nin' somewheres, but 'pears to me if there was no sinners there 'ud be no sin; an' the way to rid the univarse of sinners is to get 'em all saved or kill 'em outright."

Much more to the same effect Joe Wrag turned over in his mind that night, but we must not weary the reader with his speculations. Like many other of God's children, he was crying in the darkness and longing for light. He had found that human creeds, instead of being a ladder leading up into the temple of truth, were rather a house of bondage. Men had spread a veil before the face of God, and he had not courage to pull it aside. Now and then through the rents he caught a ray of light, but it dazzled him so that he was afraid there was something wrong about it, and he turned away his face and looked again into the darkness. And yet the night was surely passing away. It wanted but a hand to take down the shutters from the windows of his soul, and let the light – ay, and the love of God that surrounded him, like a mighty ocean – rush in. But whose hand should take down the shutters? Through what agency should the light come in? Let us wait and see.

CHAPTER VII

Two Visits

Tell me the story slowly,
That I may take it in;
That wonderful redemption,
God's remedy for sin.
Tell me the story simply,
As to a little child;
For I am weak and weary,
And helpless and defiled.

Hankey

ONE clear frosty evening early in the new year two little figures might have been seen threading their way along Old Hall Street, in the opposite direction to the Exchange. It had not long gone five, and numbers of clerks and warehousemen were crowding into the street and hurrying in the direction of their several homes. But the little figures dodged their way with great skill through the crowded street, still holding each other by the hand and keeping up most of the time a sharp trot.

After pursuing a straight course for a considerable time, they turned off suddenly to the right into a less frequented street. Then they took a turn to the left, and then again to the right. It was very evident they knew the streets well, for they wound in and out, now right, now left, without the least hesitation.

At length they reached a street where all was darkness, save where here and there the flickering rays of a candle struggled through the dirt-begrimed window. This was Bowker's Row, and Benny and his sister paused for a while before venturing into the darkness.

For several days the little hearts had been aching with curiosity to visit once more their old home. They had no wish to be seen, and as for living again in Addler's Hall, that was altogether out of the question. Still, they were filled with a curiosity that they could not resist to peep at the old spot once more, and ascertain, if possible, how far their father and stepmother were pleased or otherwise with their disappearance.

They had talked the matter over for several nights as they lay in each other's arms in the warm corner under Betty Barker's stairs. They admitted that there were difficulties, perhaps danger, in paying such a visit; but at length curiosity became too strong for them, and they resolved to risk it.

With Nelly, too, there was something more than curiosity. Notwithstanding his drunken habits and his cruelty to Benny, she loved her father, for there had been times when he had made much of her, and called her "his little Nell". Perhaps she did not love her father very deeply. In comparison to "her Benny" he occupied indeed a very third-rate place in her affections. Still he was her father, and now and then he had been kind to her, and hence he was more to her than a stranger, and her little heart longed for one more sight of his face. They did not wait long at the end of Bowker's Row. Ascertaining that the coast was tolerably clear, they darted up the street, and without anyone recognising them, turned into Addler's Hall. From the window of their late home a feeble light struggled, which satisfied them that the house was not empty.

"Take care," said Benny to his sister, "an' don't make no noise if yer can 'elp it."

"Right you are," whispered his sister, and with silent footfalls they glided up to the door and listened.

From within came the sound of voices, but they were the voices of children – strange voices, too, they were.

And Benny looked at his sister and whispered – "By golly! this are a go. The owd folks 'ave flit, that's sartin."

"Can yer get a peep through the winder, Benny?" said Nelly, with a white, startled face.

"Dunno, but I'll try." And try he did, but without success.

"Brimstone!" he whispered, scratching his head. "What's us to do? Oh, I 'ave it," he said at length. "Come 'ere, Nell. I's 'mazin' strong, an' I can lift you 'igh 'nough to get a peep."

And, taking his sister in his arms, he managed, not without considerable difficulty, to enable her to look through the window and get a glimpse of the inmates of the room.

"Do 'e know 'em, Nell?" said Benny, after he had lifted her down very carefully.

"No, I dunno who they is; I've never seen 'em afore."

"Well, then, we'll ax 'em." And without further ado he pushed open the door.

There were four hungry and neglected-looking children in the room, the oldest of them about the same age as Benny. They looked up with questioning eyes at the intruders, but said nothing.

"Does you live 'ere?" said Benny, putting on a bold face.

"Ay," was the response from all together.

"How long?" said Benny.

"Week afore last," answered the oldest lad.

"Where's the folks as lived 'ere afore you comed?"

51

"Dunno."

"Ain't you ever heerd? "

"Ay, we've heerd."

"Where is they, then?" queried Benny.

"Childer is drownded."

"Golly! Are that so?" and there was an amused twinkle in Benny's eye as he put the question.

"Ay," was the response; "we's heerd so."

"Where's their father?" was Benny's next question.

"Dunno," said the biggest lad.

"Ain't you heerd?"

"Ay, we 'ave,"

"Where is he then?"

"Well, father says he's gone to Davy Jones, but I dunno where that are."

"Nor I too," said Benny, scratching his head. Then he looked at the oldest lad again.

"Did the man's missis go wi' him, does yer know?" he inquired.

"Never heerd nothing 'bout 'er," said the lad.

"An' yer knows nothin' more 'bout 'em?"

"No, nothin'."

"Mich 'bliged," said Benny, with an air of importance. And taking Nelly by the hand, he walked out of the house.

He hardly knew whether he was most pleased or disappointed with his visit, so he said nothing to his sister until they had left Bowker's Row behind them, and got once more into the region of gaslight. Then, turning to his sister, he said, "What does yer think o' it now, Nell?"

"P'r'haps father's mended, and 'as gone to live in a better 'ouse," was the quiet reply.

"Mos' likely," said Benny, and again they trudged on in silence.

At length they paused in front of a chapel that abutted close on to the street. A few people were dropping in quietly one after another, and Benny wondered what they did inside. He had never been inside a church or a chapel; they were most of them so grand, and the people that went were dressed so well, that he had concluded long since that they were not for such poor little chaps as he. But this chapel was anything but grand-looking, and the people who were going in did not look very smart, and Benny began to wonder if he might not dare take a peep inside.

While he was speculating as to what he had better do, a gentleman who had been standing in the vestibule came out, and said in a kindly voice, "Well, my little ones, would you like to come inside?"

"May us? said Benny, eagerly.

"Oh, yes," was the reply; "we shall be very glad to see you, and there is plenty of room; come this way."

And without a word they followed him.

"Here," he said, pushing open a green baize door, "I will put you in my pew; you will be nice and comfortable there, and none of my family will be here tonight."

For a few moments the children hardly knew whether they were awake or dreaming; but at length they mustered up sufficient courage to look around them.

The place they thought was very large, but everything felt so snug and warm that they almost wished they could stay there all night. Still the people dropped in very quietly and orderly, until there were between two and three hundred present. Then a gentleman opened the organ and began to play a voluntary; softly at first, then louder, swelling out in rich full tones, then dying away again, like the sighing of a summer's breeze; anon bursting forth like the rushing of a storm, now rippling like a mountain rill, now wailing as a child in pain; now rushing on as with shouts of gladness and thanksgiving, and again dying away like the wind in far-off trees.

Nelly listened with open mouth and wondering eyes, oblivious to everything but the strains of music that were floating all around her. And Benny sat as if transfixed.

"By golly!" he whispered to Nelly, when the piece was ended. "If I ever heerd sich music as that afore. It's made me cold all over; seems to me as if someone were pouring cold water adown my back."

But Nelly answered nothing; her attention was attracted to a gentleman that stood alone on a platform with a book in his hand, Nelly thought his voice was strangely musical as he read the words –

> "Jesus, lover of my soul,
> Let me to Thy bosom fly,
> While the nearer waters roll,
> While the tempest still is high.
>
> Hide me, O my Saviour, hide,
> Till the storm of life be past;
> Safe into the haven guide:
> Oh, receive my soul at last."

Then all the people stood up to sing, and the children thought they had never heard anything half so sweet before. Great tears welled up in Nelly's brimming eyes and rolled down her cheeks; though if anyone had asked her why she wept, she would not have been able to tell.

Then followed a prayer full of devout thanksgiving and of earnest pleading. Then came another hymn –

> "Would Jesus have a sinner die?
> Why hangs He then on yonder tree?
> What means that strange expiring cry?
> Sinners, He prays for you and me:
> Forgive them, Father, oh! forgive;
> They know not that by Me they live."

And once more the congregation stood up to sing. Nelly was even more affected than during the singing of the previous hymn, and while they sang the last verse ...

> "Oh, let me kiss His bleeding feet,
> And bathe and wash them with my tears,
> The story of His love repeat
> In every drooping sinner's ears,
> That all may hear the quick'ning sound,
> Since I, even I, have mercy found,"

... she fairly broke down, and, hiding her face in her hands, she sobbed aloud.

She soon recovered herself, however, when the preacher began to speak. Clear and distinct his words rang out, "Let the wicked forsake his ways, and the unrighteous man his thoughts, and let him return unto the Lord, and He will have mercy upon him; and to our God, for He will abundantly pardon."

And Nelly eagerly drank in his words as he went on to tell how we were all wanderers from our Father's house; and how the Father's heart yearned towards us, and how He had invited all to return home, giving the same invitation to every one of His children, and promising an abundant pardon to all that would come. And then he told, by way of illustration, the beautiful parable of the Prodigal Son, and concluded with an earnest exhortation to all the unsaved to come to the Saviour that very night, and to come just as they were.

Nelly felt that she would very much like to "come to the Saviour", but, alas! she did not know how. And when she saw several persons leave their pews and kneel around the communion, she wondered if they were "prodigals going home to the Father".

But what of Benny? Alas! if Joe Wrag had seen him that evening, he would have been more than ever convinced that he was none of the elect, and that he had not one particle of spiritual discernment. The words of the preacher seemed to have a very soothing influence upon our hero, for scarcely had he uttered twenty words of the sermon ere Benny was fast asleep. Nor did he wake again till near the end of the service, when he was startled by a strange voice speaking.

It was one of the men that Nelly had noticed kneeling at the communion. The man stood up, and with a face radiant with his new-found joy, he said in broken accents, "Oh, friends, thank the Lord for me, for I have found the Saviour!"

Evidently he intended to have said more, but overcome by his emotion, he sat down and hid his face in his hands.

"I'm glad the chap found 'im," said Benny to his sister, as they hurried homeward, "for he seemed desp'rate cut up 'bout it."

But Nelly did not answer, she was too full of what she had seen, and heard, and felt, to speak.

The next evening, long before service-time, they were waiting around the chapel door, and when at length the door was opened, they were welcomed by the same gentleman that had spoken to them the previous evening, and put into the same pew. And once more was Benny delighted with the music, and once more was he soothed to sleep by the sermon.

But not so Nelly. As the preacher explained that wonderful text, "For God so loved the world, that He gave His only begotten Son, that whosoever believeth in Him, might not perish, but have everlasting life," she seemed to see more clearly what the preacher meant than on the previous night. And while he dwelt on the word 'whosoever', she felt that she was included in this invitation of mercy. In fact, it seemed to her as if a great deal the preacher had said had been for her special benefit, and that for her the Saviour had provided a home more beautiful than any of the pictures she had seen in Joe Wrag's fire.

As they were leaving, near the close of the service, a young gentleman placed his hand on Benny's shoulder, and said, "Well, my little man, I hope you have found the Saviour."

"Lor' a massy!" said Benny, with a look of surprise upon his face. "Are that little chap lost agin? He can't be well looked arter, that's sartin."

"You don't understand," said the young man; "but perhaps I should have asked if the Saviour has found you?"

"Not that I knows on," said Benny, stoutly. "Nobody finds me, I finds myself."

"Dear me!" said the young man, "you mistake my meaning altogether."

"Does I?"

"Yes, my little fellow. But I will talk with you again some other time, when there is more time."

"Will yer?"

"Yes; but now good night."

"Good night," said Benny and Nelly in chorus, and once more they left the warm house of prayer for the cold and wintry street.

"You would understand better, Benny," said his sister, as they journeyed homeward, "if yer would listen to granny, an' not go to sleep whiles the man is talkin'."

"Dunno that I should, Nell. I's not 'cute 'bout those things like you is; but let's 'urry on, for I's gettin' as cold as Jonar in the den o' lions."

Benny was very fond of Old Testament stories, and granny had humoured his liking in this respect, but the way he mixed up the prophets, patriarchs, and other noted Bible characters, was rather bewildering.

"Never mind," he would say, when granny took him to task on this matter, "so long's I gets hold o' the right hend o' the story, mixin' up the names a bit makes no matter, as fur as I can see."

So granny let him have his way, concluding that he would mend in that matter as he got older.

"But," the old woman would say, "he'll never be like little Nelly. Bless her! I's afeard, sometimes, she's too good an' knowin' to live."

CHAPTER VIII

In Which Joe Wrag Has a Vision

They are going, only going,
Jesus called them long ago;
All the wintry time they're passing
Softly as the falling snow.

When the violets in the spring-time
Catch the azure of the sky,
They are carried out to slumber
Sweetly where the violets lie.

AS winter slowly wore away, little Nelly's health began to fail. She seemed weary and languid, and poor little Benny was at his wits' end to know what to get her to eat. After spending more than he could really afford in something that he thought would tempt her appetite, he was grieved beyond measure when she would turn away her head and say, "I's very sorry for yer, Benny, but I canna eat it; I would if I could."

And he would be compelled reluctantly to eat it himself; though he would not mind going without food altogether if only little Nell could eat. But he comforted himself with the thought that she would get better when the spring-time came, and the streets were dry and warm. He might get her into the parks, too, and she would be sure, he thought, to get an appetite then. And so he kept up his spirits, and hoped for the best.

"She's ripenin' for the kingdom," was Joe Wrag's reflection, as he watched her pale face becoming thinner, and her great round eyes becoming larger and more luminous day by day. "She belongs to the elect, there ken be no doubt, an' the Lord don't intend for her little bare feet to walk the cold, dirty streets o' Liverpool much longer. I reckon she'll soon be walking the golden streets o' the shinin' city, where there's no more cold, nor hunger, nor pain. I shall be main sorry to lose her, bless her little heart, for I'm feared there's no chance of me ever seein' her agin' when she's gone. I wonder if the Lord would permit me to look at her through the bars o' the gate just for a minit, if I wur to ax Him very hard? 'T will be nice, anyhow, to think o' her bein' comforted while I'm tormented. But it comes 'ard 'pon such as us as don't belong to the elect, whichever way we looks at it."

Sometimes Joe would leave his home earlier in the afternoon than usual, and getting a nice bunch of grapes, he would make his way towards Nelly's stand as the short winter's day was fading in the west. He would rarely have much difficulty in finding his little pet, and taking her up in his great strong arms, he would carry her off through bye-streets to his hut. And wrapping her in his great warm overcoat, and placing her on a low seat that he had contrived for her, he would leave her to enjoy her grapes, while he went out to light the fire and see that the lamps were properly set for the night.

With a dreamy look in her eyes, Nelly would watch her old friend kindling his fire and putting things 'ship-shape', as he termed it, and would think how well she had been cared for of late.

By-and-bye, when the fire crackled and glowed in the grate, Joe would come into the hut and take her upon his knee, and she would lean her head against his shoulder with

60

a heart more full of thankfulness than words of hers could utter. And at such times, at her request, Joe would tell her of the mercy that was infinite, and of the love that was stronger than death. She had only been twice to the chapel, for when she and Benny went the following week they discovered that there was no service, and so disappointed were they that they had not gone again; for the chapel was a long distance from Tempest Court, and she was tired when the day's work was done, and to go such a long distance and find the doors closed was anything but inviting. So they had not ventured again. But Nelly had heard enough from granny and while at the chapel to make her thirst for more. And so Joe became her teacher, and evening by evening, whenever opportunity presented, he unfolded to her the "old, old story of Jesus and His love".

It made his heart ache, though, to talk of the "good tidings of great joy," and think they were not for him. If the truth must be told, this was the reason why he kept away from church and chapel. He had adopted in early life the Calvinistic creed, and had come to the conclusion, when about thirty years of age, that he belonged to the 'eternally reprobate'. Hence, to go to church to listen to promises that were not for him, to hear offers of salvation that he could not accept, to be told of a heaven that he could never enter, and of a hell that he could not shun, was more than his sensitive nature could bear.

And yet, as he repeated to Nelly the wonderful promises of the Gospel, they seemed sometimes to widen out, until they embraced the whole world, including even him, and for a moment his heart would throb with joy and hope. Then again the bossy front of his creed would loom up before him like an iron wall, hiding the light, shutting out the sunshine, and leaving him still in 'outer darkness'.

One day Nelly rather startled him by saying, in her sweet

childish way, "I does like that word who-so-ever!"

"Do you?" said Joe.

"Oh, yes, very much; don't you?"

"Well, I 'ardly knows what to make on it."

"How is that, Joe?" said Nelly, looking up with a wondering expression on her face.

"Well, 'cause it seems to mean what it don't mean," said Joe, jerking out the words with an effort. "Oh, no, Joe; how can that be?"

"Well, that's jist where I'm floored, Nelly. But it seem to be the fact, anyhow."

"Oh, Joe! And would the Saviour you've been a-tellin' me of say what He didna mean?" And a startled expression came over the child's face, as if the ground was slipping from beneath her.

"No, no, Nelly, He could not say that; but the pinch is about what the word do mean."

"Oh, the man in the chapel said it meaned everybody, an' I reckon he knows, 'cause he looked as if he wur sartin."

"Did he, Nelly? Then perhaps he wur right."

"Oh, yes, it's everybody, Joe. I feels as if it wur so inside."

"Purty little hangel!" said Joe, in an undertone. "But there is somethin' in the Book about 'out of the mouths of babes an' sucklings.' I'll read it again when I gets home."

That night, as Joe Wrag sat in his hut alone, while the silence of the slumbering town was unbroken, save for the echoing footfall of the policeman on his beat, he seemed to see the iron wall of his creed melt and vanish, till not a shred remained, and beyond where it stood stretched endless plains of light and glory. And arching the sky from horizon to horizon, a rainbow glowed of every colour and hue, and in the rainbow a promise was written in letters of fire, and as he gazed the letters burst forth into brighter flame, and the promise was this, "Whosoever cometh unto me, I will in no wise cast them out." And over the distant hills a great multitude appeared in sight – so many, indeed, that he could not number them. But he noticed this, that none of them were sick, or feeble, or old. No touch of pain was on any face, no line of care on any brow, and nearer and yet nearer they came, till he could hear the regular tramp, tramp of their feet, and catch the words they were chanting as if with one voice. How thankful he was that the great town was hushed and still, so that he could not mistake the words. "And the Spirit and the Bride say, Come. And let him that heareth say, Come. And let him that is athirst come. And whosoever will, let him take the water of life freely." And still nearer their echoing footfalls came, when suddenly the glowing arch of fire in his grate fell together, and a policeman passing his hut with measured tread, shouted, "Good night, Joe. We shall have a storm, I reckon; the wind has got up terrible during the last hour."

"Ay, ay," responded Joe, rubbing his eyes and wondering for a moment what had come over him.

"You seem hardly awake, Joe," laughed the policeman.

"Believe I 'ave nodded a bit," said Joe. "But, bless me, how the wind do howl!"

"Yes, it'll be rough outside the 'bar,' I reckon. I hope we shall have no wrecks. Good night."

"Good night," said Joe, as he staggered out of his hut to mend the fire, which done, he sat down to reflect.

"Wur it a vision?" he soliloquised, "or wur it a dream, or wur it 'magination? Wur it given to teach or to mislead me? But, lor', how bright that promise did shine! I ken see it now. It are in the Bible, too, that's the queerest part on it. An' how beautiful they did sing, an' how they did shout out that part, 'Whosoever will'. Lor' bless us! I can't get it out

63

o' my noddle; nor I dunno that I want to, it's so amazin' comfortin', and much more nearer my idear of what God ought to be, 'cause as how there is no limit to it."

And Joe scratched his head vigorously, which was a sure sign that some new idea had struck him.

"Well, bang me!" he ejaculated, "if I ain't floored again. Ain't God infinite? an' if that be the case He must be infinite 'all round.' An' that bein' so, then His power's infinite, an' His marcy's infinite, an' His love's infinite, an' He's all infinite. No limit to nothin'. An' if that be so, it don't square nohow with His love an' marcy stoppin' just at the point where the elect leaves off an' the reprobate begins."

And Joe took a long iron rod and stirred up the fire until it roared again, muttering to himself the while. "Well, if I ain't completely banged. I'll ax little Nell. I b'lieve she knows more about it now than I do, by a long chalk."

By this time slates and chimneypots began to drop around him in a decidedly dangerous fashion, and he had again to seek the shelter of his hut. But even there he did not feel quite safe, for the little wooden house rocked and creaked in the might of the storm, and threatened to topple over altogether.

There was no longer any chance of meditation, so he had to content himself listening to the roar of the storm. Sometimes he heard its voice moaning away in the distant streets, and he wondered where it had gone to. Then he heard it coming up behind his hut again, at first quietly, as if meditating what to do; then it would gather strength and speed, and he would listen as it came nearer and nearer, till it would rush shrieking past his hut, making it creak and shiver, and once more there would be a momentary lull.

And so Joe waited and listened through the wild solemn night, and longed as he had rarely done for the light of the morning to appear.

CHAPTER IX

Tempted

Where the watching, waiting angels
Lead them from the shadow dim,
To the brightness of His presence
Who has called them unto Him,
Little hearts for ever stainless,
Little hands as pure as they,
Little feet by angels guided,
Never a forbidden way.

TOWARDS the close of February Nelly caught a very severe cold, which kept her indoors for several days. One night her cough had been so bad that she had scarcely slept at all, and when she got up in the morning, with flushed cheeks and hollow eyes, unrested and unrefreshed, granny insisted that she was not fit to go out, and that she must stay indoors and keep herself warm.

Benny was very sorry to lose her earnings, for, alas! it had been a hard struggle for the children to find the necessary coppers day by day to purchase food and pay far their lodgings; and had it not been for Joe Wrag's kindness, they would often have fared much worse. Nelly knew this very well, and hence it was a great trial to her to stay indoors doing nothing, while her Benny was out fighting the world alone.

"How will yer manage, Benny?" she said, with an anxious

look in her eyes, the first morning that he went out alone.

"Oh, 'never fear, Nell, I'll 'cumulate the coppers somehow," was the response.

"What's 'cumulate, Benny?" for it was the first time he had ventured to use that word in her hearing.

"Well, I might a-knowed," he said, putting on a knowing look, "that you would not hundercumstand sich words, 'cause as how you don't seem to care for larnin' like me."

"Well, you 'ave not told me now, Benny."

"Oh, it means as how I'm bound to get the coppers somehow."

"How *somehow*, Benny? You'll only get 'em the right way, will yer, now?"

"Never fear, Nell; I's not goin' to steal 'em."

"But if you dunna get enough, Benny?"

"Oh, I'll go hungry for a day or two; 't won't be fust time I's done it."

"Poor Benny!" and she placed her wasted hand on his shoulder. "But I 'ope it will be true, what Joe told me t'other night."

"What did he tell yer?"

"Well, he said the good Lord was sure to provide; that is, you know, Benny, He willna let us starve."

"I dunno much about *Him*, Nell."

"Oh, but Joe 'as told me lot an' lots about Him; an' He never says what He doesna mean; an' if He says He'll provide, He will, Benny."

"Anynow, I shall be glad to see it," was Benny's observation, as he walked away, leaving Nelly standing at the door.

He found the days very long without a sight of his sister's face from morn till eve. But he bore up bravely, and hurried home as early as he possibly could when the day's toil was over. Nobody knew how much "little Nell" was to him: she had been the only comfort of his cheerless life, and when the world seemed more rough and unfriendly than usual, it was Nelly who stood by his side like a ministering angel, encouraging him still to persevere.

The sight of her sweet patient face in the evening was like a benediction to him, and after the frugal meal they would sit on the floor with their arms around each other before granny's fire. And Benny would tell his sister all the experiences of the day; making light, however, of the difficulties and disappointment, and magnifying every little pleasure that had fallen to his lot.

It was wonderful how thoughtful he was of his sister, and how he anticipated her every want. He would not give her a moment's pain on any consideration if he could possibly help it. Yet Nelly always knew when he was in trouble, though he said nothing about it; for experience had made her quick to detect his every mood.

One afternoon, as Benny was passing along a narrow and not very frequented street, he paused before a small hosier's shop. A great many things had been hung outside the door to catch the eye of the passer-by. But one article especially attracted his attention, and that was a woollen "cross-over."

"Golly!" he said to himself, "if Nelly only had that, she'd be better in no time."

Nelly had been much better that morning, and but for the keen east wind that had been blowing for several days, she would have again ventured into the streets. And as Benny looked agin and again at the cross-over, he thought how nice she would look with it crossed over her chest, and how nice and snug and warm it would make her feel. No cold, he was sure, could come through a thing like that; and it was the cold, granny said, that made her cough so much.

But he knew he could not purchase it, so with a sigh he turned away. Yet in less than half an hour he was standing before the shop again.

"They would never miss it," he muttered to himself, "an' Nelly needs it so much."

Then a voice within him whispered, "Don't steal, Benny," and again he walked away. But the tempter followed and gave him no rest.

"I could cut the string as easy as that," he said to himself, snapping his fingers. "And it ain't for myself that I wants it, and I dunna think it can be so very wrong to take it for little Nell, when she's so ill."

While he was musing thus, he was startled by a voice near him, "Hullo, Ben, are 'e goin' to a funeral, yer look so glum?"

Looking up a narrow entry, he saw a lad that went by the name of "Perks," engaged in trying on a pair of shoes, that were evidently new, though they had been well plastered with mud.

Perks was not so big as Benny, though he was two or three years older. He was a strange-looking lad. A great shock of fiery red hair made hat or cap totally unnecessary. His face was plain, looked at under any circumstances, but a look of low cunning made it at times appear almost repulsive.

Perks was no friend of Benny's, who rarely took the trouble to reply when addressed by him. Benny knew that he was not honest. He never sold matches, and rarely carried parcels, and yet he had generally plenty of coppers at his disposal, and wore better clothes than any of the street lads. But today Benny was in a different humour to what he was generally. He had permitted an evil spirit to take possession of him, and so was not so particular about his company. So he walked up the entry close to where

Perks sat, and pointing to the shoes, said in a whisper, "Where 'd yer get them?"

"Walked 'em," was the response.

"That is, stole 'em, ain't it?"

"Gem'mem of our per-fession don't say stole, it ain't perlite," said Perks, trying to look important.

"It means that, though," said Benny.

"Well, I admit I took 'em without leave, as I takes most things; it's most conwenient."

"How did yer manage?" said Benny.

"So yer wants to take up the perfession, does yer?" And there was a cunning leer in his eye as he spoke.

"No, I don't," said Benny, colouring up.

"What yer ax me for 'ow I did it, then?"

"For fun."

"No doubt. But, I'll tell yer, nothin' is easier. Folks hang things outside on purpose to be stole. I took up the per-fession 'cause I couldn't 'elp it. Shopkeepers put things right under my nose, an' made me take 'em against my will at fust. Now I's no feelin' 'bout it at all."

"'T ain't right, though, nohow," said Benny.

Perks was about to sneer at this remark, but thought better of it, and answered, after a pause, "Well, if it ain't, I's not to blame. Folks just put things in my way; an' a chap's not to blame for eatin' butter when it's put in his mouth."

To this Benny ventured no remark. And Perks having fastened on the shoes to his satisfaction, said, "Come with me a minute," and together they walked off into a more crowded thoroughfare.

Poor Benny! in such a state of mind as he was, he could not have fallen into worse hands. He was fast getting into the toils of the tempter; and who should deliver him?

For a while Benny and Perks walked on in silence, when

suddenly Perks clutched his arm and whispered in his ear, "Look alive, an' I'll show yer a bit of nice play."

"What yer mean?" said Benny.

"Yer see that man afore us, with a bit o' his hankercher peepin' out o' his pocket?"

"Ay"

"Well, there 's another chap walkin' alongside o' him, an' comin' down the street is three or four more; don't 'e see as how they'll all meet by that lamp-post? Well, ther'll be a bit o' crush, an' I'll just pop in atween 'em at the same time onexpected, an' for a moment we'll be sixes an' sevens, an' then the thing is done."

And off Perks darted like the wind. Benny did not wait to see how he succeeded in his undertaking. The poisonous seed had taken root in the soil that had been prepared for its reception, and Benny hurried away to the hosier's shop, alas! already a thief in heart, if not in action, for he had made up his mind to take the crossover if anything like a favourable opportunity presented itself.

"I's not to blame for takin' things," he said, using Perks's words, "if people puts 'em right in one's way."

It was getting dusk, and in this narrow street it was darker than in the street he had just left.

Yes, there was the crossover. And, after looking at all the windows in the neighbourhood, to see that no one was watching him, he glided stealthily up to the door. The shopkeeper was busy inside. "So much the better," he thought. "Now's the time. And he stretched out his hand to grasp the coveted article, when a hand was laid upon his arm with a firm grip, and, turning, he saw a face that made the perspiration ooze from him at every pore.

Leaving Benny for a moment to recover his fright, we will go back to Tempest Court, and have a look at Nelly. She had been restless and ill at ease all the day – a sign, granny said, that she was getting better; and, indeed, she felt much better in body, though she was uneasy in mind, and, as the day kept fine and got much warmer as the hours wore on, she determined she would go out and see how Benny was getting on, for she had a vague presentiment that all was not right.

On reaching the landing-stage she looked anxiously around, but Benny was nowhere visible. This did not trouble her much, but after loitering around for a good part of an hour, and he did not come, she began to feel alarmed; still she waited around, till, unable longer to bear the burden of suspense, she started off to search for him. Up one street and down another she went, looking here and there and everywhere, but without avail.

Just before four o'clock she made her way to the old trysting-place by St. George's Church, in the hope that Benny might do the same; but, alas! she was doomed to disappointment, for he did not come; and when she saw the daylight begin to fade, she got frightened, feeling sure that some evil had be-fallen "her Benny."

Evil, alas! had befallen him, though not of the nature she had feared.

At length she saw someone turn up a narrow street that looked like Benny. She could not be certain, but she would follow and see; so with beating heart she hurried up the street.

Yes, it was Benny; she was near enough to recognise him now. But when she saw – as she did at a glance – what he was about to do, her heart stood still for a moment; the next moment she hurried forward with the fleetness of the wind, and laid her hand upon his arm, unable to speak a word.

For two or three seconds the children looked at each

other in silence, then Nelly took her brother by the hand and led him away. She uttered no word of reproach, she only said, "My poor Benny!" and her great round eyes filled with tears, which rolled silently down her wasted cheeks.

"It was for you, Nelly. I thought 't would warm yer. I wouldna 'ave done it for myself."

And again came the words, in a choking voice, "My poor Benny!"

"I didna think it wur so very wicked, seein' as you is so ill, Nelly. Is you very mad at me, Nell?"

"I's not mad, Benny, but I's sorry – oh, so sorry! I did not think – "

But here she broke off abruptly: she would utter no word of reproach, for she knew it was all out of love for her.

That evening she could eat no supper. Benny knew the reason and did not press her, but her silent grief nearly broke his heart. He would rather suffer anything himself than see his sister suffer. And yet now he had given her keener pain than words could tell.

In the middle of the night he awoke and found her sobbing by his side as though her little heart would break, and he knew that he was the cause of her grief.

"Don't take on so, Nell," he said, in a voice that had the sound of tears in it. And he drew her tear-stained face towards him and kissed her affectionately.

But she only sobbed the more.

"Do forgive me, Nell," he said. "I's very sorry."

"I 'as nothin' to forgive you for, Benny; you's always been good to me. Ax the dear Lord to forgive yer."

"I knows nowt about Him, Nell."

"But He knows about you, Benny – Joe says so; and He sees everything we does. Ax Him."

"Could He hear if I wur to ax Him?"

"Yes, Joe says as He hears everything."

"Then I'll try Him," said Benny, and, sitting up in bed, he commenced, "If you plaise, Mr. God, I's very sorry I tried to stole; but if you'll be a trump an' not split on a poor little chap, I'll be mighty 'bliged to yer. An' I promise 'e I won't do nowt o' the sort agin."

"There, will that do, Nell?"

"Say Amen."

"Amen," said Benny, and he lay down to listen for the answer.

But after waiting a long time and no voice broke the stillness of the night, and Nelly having fallen asleep, our hero concluded that *she* had received the answer, as she seemed so much comforted; so he thought that he might go to sleep also, which he accordingly did, and did not awake till late in the morning, when he saw his sister bending over him with a calm face from which all trace of pain had fled, and a beautiful light shining in her eyes.

This satisfied him that his prayer had been answered, and once more his heart was at peace.

CHAPTER X

In the Woods

I roam the woods that crown
The upland, where the mingled splendours glow,
Where the gay company of trees look down
On the green fields below.

Let in through all the trees
Come the strange rays; the forest depths are bright,
Their sunny-coloured foliage in the breeze
Twinkles like beams of light.

Bryant

PERKS was very much annoyed that Benny had not stayed to see him perform the feat of picking a gentleman's pocket, nevertheless, he was very anxious to cultivate our hero's acquaintance, especially as Benny had generally treated him with unmistakable contempt; so on the following morning he sought out Benny, and tried his very best to make himself agreeable. But Benny was in a decidedly unfriendly mood, and threw cold water on all Perks' advances. But, nothing daunted, Perks kept near him most of the day, and even offered to treat him to what he called 'a feed'. But it was of no use. Benny had learned a lesson he would not easily forget, and he knew that his safety lay in having as little to do with Perks and his class as possible. So as evening came on and Perks still hung around him, he lost all patience, and, doubling his fist in an unmistakable manner, he said, with a gymnastic flourish, "Look 'ere, Perks, if yer don't walk yer pegs in double-quick time, you'll wish yer had, that's all."

"Oh, that's yer game, is it?" said Perks, in a defiant tone, and squaring up in front of Benny.

"It are," was the reply; "an' if yer don't want to see fire, you'd better be off like greased lightnin'."

"I shall go when I likes, and not afore," said Perks; "an' if yer thinks yer's goin' to bully this little chap, you's got the wrong pig by the ear."

"I wants to bully nobody," said Benny, in a milder tone; "but I won't have yer a-hangin' about me all day."

"I'spose yer wants to crib somethin' without my knowin' it," said Perks, with a sneer.

"It's a lie," said Benny, colouring painfully, as the event of the previous day crossed his mind.

"'T ain't a lie, neither," was the response, "or you'd not get so red over it."

"D' yer think I's a thief, then?" said Benny.

"No," said Perks scornfully, "but I knows it."

"An' yer shall know some'at else afore yer a minit older," said Benny, springing upon him, and dealing him a blow between the eyes that made him stagger, and, before he could recover himself, a second blow sent him reeling against a wall.

For a moment Perks glared at his antagonist with flaming eyes, but he saw that he was no match for Benny, so he turned on his heel and walked away. He had not gone many steps, however, before he came back again.

"Look here, Ben Bates," he said, "you's licked me now, but I'll get my revenge, an' I'll a'most plague the life out o' yer," and once more he walked away.

Perks kept his word; from that day he became the greatest plague of Benny's life. He stole his matches, picked his pocket, tripped him up in the street, and annoyed him in every possible way that he could imagine, always mindful, however, to keep out of the reach of Benny's arm; and, being fleet-footed, that was not difficult.

Benny, however, said that he could "'ford to bide his time," so he quietly went on his way, feeling that nothing could trouble him very much now that "little Nell" was getting better again.

And as the summer advanced she did seem to get very much better. The cough became less troublesome, her appetite improved, her cheerfulness came back, and altogether she seemed to be taking, as Joe Wrag put it, "a new lease of her life."

And yet a close observer would have noticed that the improvement was more in appearance than in reality. The pink spot still burned on either cheek, and her great round eyes shone with an unnatural lustre, and her strength, which had been failing for months, did not seem to come back; and though she went out with Benny in the morning and came back with him in the evening, yet each evening she seemed more tired and worn than on the previous one. She made no complaint, however; but, on the contrary, always declared that she was getting ever so much better.

For several weeks Joe Wrag had been planning to give the children a treat; and one fine morning in June he put in an appearance at Tempest Court before they had left, much to their surprise and delight.

Nelly was the first to see him coming up the court, and ran to meet him, her eyes beaming with pleasure. "Oh, Joe," she exclaimed, "I's so pleased to see you!"

"Is you, my purty?" said Joe, fondly; and, stooping down,

he took her up in his arms, and carried her into the house.

Granny looked up in surprise, and Benny stared in bewilderment, fearing there was mischief in the wind.

"Yer don't get much heavier," said Joe, sitting down with Nelly on his knee. "We'll have to feed yer up a bit somehow."

"Oh, I's very well, Joe," said Nelly, nestling closer to her old friend.

"Dunno 'bout that," said Joe, reflectively; "but what d' yer say 'bout havin' holiday today?"

"Oh, Methusaler!" said Benny, brightening up in a moment, "that's the game, are it?" and he went out in the doorway and stood on his head – a sure sign that he was more than usually delighted.

Nelly looked up in Joe's face with a beautiful light in her eyes. "D'yer mean it, Joe?" she said, simply.

"Ay, my bonny, that I do," responded Joe.

"Oh, then, won't it be jist – jist – "

"Profusely," said Benny, coming to her rescue with one of his grand words, of which he had been laying in a stock of late.

"Now, then," said Joe, "get on yer best togs, and let's be off."

Poor children! they had not much of best or worst in the way of attire, but, such as it was, it was clean and neatly mended. Granny did her very best to turn them out respectable, and certainly they did her no discredit.

"Where is we going?" said Nelly, as she stepped along by Joe's side, her eyes sparkling with delight.

"Into the woods somewhere on t' other side o' the water," said Joe, looking fondly down into the child's beaming eyes.

Benny had nearly stood on his head again when he heard

that; but thought better of it, and contented himself with a shrill whistle expressive of delight.

Better an' better," he thought, flinging his cap into the air and catching it on his toe; "won't I enjoy myself, just, that's all?"

By ten o'clock they were on the landing-stage, and soon after they were gliding up the river towards Eastham. Oh, how the wavelets sparkled in the summer's sunshine, and how the paddle-wheels tossed the water into foam. How happy everything seemed today! The ferries were crowded with passengers, all of whom seemed in the best of spirits; and the rush of water and the beat of the engine seemed to Nelly the happiest sounds she had ever heard.

Benny was rushing here and there and everywhere, and asking Joe questions about everything. But Nelly sat still. Her thoughts were too big for utterance, and her little heart was full to overflowing.

At length they reach New Ferry, where several passengers get off and several others get on; then on they glide again. The river here seems like a sheet of glass, so broad and smooth. Now they are nearing the river's bank, and Nelly is delighted to watch the trees gliding past. How wonderful everything seems! Surely her dreams are becoming a reality at last.

For a while after they land they sit on the river's bank in the shade of the trees, and Nelly rubs her eyes and pinches herself, to be certain that she is not asleep. How grandly the mile-wide river at their feet flows downward to the sea! And what a beautiful background to the picture the wooded landscape makes that stretches away beyond Garston and Aigburth! And Nelly wonders to herself if it is possible that heaven can be more beautiful than this.

But Benny soon gets impatient to be off up the wood,

and, humouring his wish, they set off up the narrow path, between banks of ferns and primroses and wild flowers of almost every hue. The tall trees wave their branches above them, and the birds whistle out their happy hearts. Here and there the grass-hoppers chirp among the undergrowth, and myriads of insects make the air vocal with their ceaseless hum.

They had scarcely got into the heart of the wood ere they found that Benny was missing; but they were neither surprised nor alarmed at this, for the lad was fairly brimming over with delight, and could not stay for five minutes in the same place if he were to be crowned.

Nelly was as much delighted as her brother; perhaps more so, but she had a different way of expressing it. She felt as she sat on a mossy bank, holding Joe's rough and horny hand within both her own, and looked away up the long avenues between the trees, and watched the dancing sunlight that was sifted down in golden patches, and listened to the dreamy murmur of the summer's wind through the leafy trees, mingling with the song of birds and the lowing of the cattle in the distant fields, as if she could have cried for very joy. It was all so solemn, and yet so delightful, so awe-inspiring and yet so gladsome, that she hardly knew whether to laugh outright, or hide her face on Joe's shoulder and have a good cry.

Benny, however, decided the matter for her. He had been wandering no one knew whither, and Joe was beginning to think that it was time to go off in search of him, when they heard him shouting at the top of his voice, "Joe, Joe! Golly! Make haste – quick, d' ye hear? Thunder!"

Judging by the tone of his voice, as well as by his words, that he was in a difficulty of some kind, Joe and Nelly started off in the direction from whence the sound came.

79

They had not gone far, however, before they espied our hero, and at sight of him Joe stood stock-still and held his sides. For there was Benny suspended by his nether garment to the branch of a tree, and striking out with his hands and feet like a huge octopus in a frantic and vain endeavour to recover a horizontal position.

He had gone out on this branch, which was not more than six feet from the ground, for some unknown purpose, and, missing his hold, he slipped, and would have fallen to the ground but for the friendly stump that held him suspended in mid-air.

"Joe! Oh, do come! Murder and turf! D' ye hear? What's yer larfin at? Are 'e moon-struck? Oh – h – !" he shrieked out at the top of his voice, still going through most unheard-of gymnastic exercises, and vainly trying to raise his head to the level of his heels.

To make the matter worse, a young gentleman passing at the time inquired of Benny, with a very grave face, "Whether his was a new method of learning to swim on dry land? If so, he thought he had got the action nearly perfect, the only thing required was to keep his head just a trifle higher."

By this time, however, Joe had come to his relief, and easily lifted him down without further mishap.

The young gentleman tried to poke some more fun at Benny, but he would not reply, and soon after set off with Joe and Nelly to get some dinner. After dinner they took a ramble across the fields, in the direction of Raby Mere Benny's adventure had rather sobered him, so he did not object to assist his sister in gathering wild flowers, while Joe artistically arranged them into what seemed to the children to be a magnificent bouquet.

Fleet-footed indeed were the hours of that long summer's

afternoon. Benny wished a thousand times that the day could last for ever; and Nelly, though she was getting tired, watched with a look of pain in her eyes the sun getting farther and farther down in the western sky.

As they were returning across the fields Benny was strongly tempted to leap a ditch that he had noticed at the beginning of their ramble – so strongly tempted indeed that he could not resist it. So off he set at a swinging trot as soon as they got into the field. Joe guessed what he was after, and called him back; but it was of no use, he either did not hear or would not heed, for he went faster and faster as he neared the ditch. Joe saw him fling up his hands, take a flying leap, and then disappear. After waiting a few moments, and he did not appear on the opposite bank, Joe and Nelly hurried after him. On reaching the ditch they found that he was stuck fast in the mud about two feet from the opposite side, and the more he tried to get out the deeper he sank.

"Oh, quick, Joe!" he shouted, "or I'll be out o' sight in another minit."

"Sarve you right!" said Joe, laughing; "you had no business to get in there."

"I can't stay to argify," retorted Benny; "don't yer see there's scarce anything of me left?"

"Ay, I see plain enough," said Joe, going to the other side, and pulling him out, though not without an effort. "I wonder what mischief you'll be into next?"

"Dunno," said Benny, regarding his legs with a look of dismay. Then, after a long pause, "I say, Joe, how's I to get this mud off?"

"Scrape off what yer can," said Joe, "and let the rest dry, and it'll rub off as clean as a new pin."

Benny was rather ashamed of his appearance, however, when he got into the wood again, and found himself in the midst of two or three hundred Sunday-school children and their teachers, all nicely dressed, who had come out for a picnic. But when he saw them each with a small bun loaf and a cup of milk, he could not help drawing near, notwithstanding the rather disgraceful state of his legs. Nelly was also anxious to have a nearer view of all those happy-looking children.

Fortunately for Benny, the superintendent of the school was the gentleman that had invited him into the chapel months before. Benny felt sure he knew them again, but whether he did or not, he invited all three to sit down with the rest, and gave them each a bun and a cup of milk.

Joe was as delighted as the children with the kindness shown, and was soon quite at his ease.

After lunch the children ran races for prizes, and Benny was invited to compete with the rest. This suited him exactly, and very soon after, with about a dozen others, he was bounding up a broad avenue between the trees, in a well-matched and most exciting race.

For the first half of the distance Benny dropped into the rear, then he began gradually to gain upon the others. Now was his time, so putting on a spurt, for which he had saved his breath, he went bounding ahead of all the others, and amid loud hurrahs came first into the goal.

Benny never felt so proud in his life before as when that first prize – a brand new sixpence – was put into his hand. His success, however, disqualified him from competing again, so he had to content himself with watching the others run.

But the most delightful circumstance of all to Nelly was when all the children stood up in a large circle, and sang in their pure young voices the following hymn:

> "Land ahead! Its fruits are waving
> O'er the fields of fadeless green;
> And the living waters laving
> Shores where heavenly forms are seen.
>
> "There let go the anchor. Riding
> On this calm and silvery bay,
> Seaward fast the tide is gliding,
> Shores in sunlight stretch away.
>
> "Now we're safe from all temptation,
> All the storms of life are past;
> Praise the Rock of our salvation,
> We are safely home at last."

Nelly never forgot that little hymn to her dying day; and when that evening they glided down the placid river towards home, she repeated to herself over and over again.

> "Seaward fast the tide is gliding,
> Shores in sunlight stretch away."

And when in her little corner she lay down to sleep, it was only to dream of the sunlit shores on the banks of the far Jordan river.

Heaven seemed nearer and dearer to her ever after that day, and she sometimes almost longed for the sunny slopes of that far-off country where there should be no more weariness nor pain.

CHAPTER XI

Benny Prays

Prayer is the burden of a sigh,
The falling of a tear,
The upward glancing of the eye
When none but God is near.

Prayer is the simplest form of speech
That infant lips can try;
Prayer the sublimest strains that reach
The Majesty on high.

Montgomery

THE long summer days passed all too quickly, and autumn came again. The days began to shorten, and the evenings to be cold. Nelly felt the change in an unmistakable manner, for her cough returned worse than ever, and her appetite and strength began to fail rapidly. But the hopeful little child battled bravely with her growing weakness, and each morning went forth to earn her daily bread.

One afternoon in October Benny was down on the pier, when he saw Perks coming towards him, and not wishing to have anything to say to him, he was about to turn away, when Perks called out, "Does yer want to hear a bit o' news?"

"No!" said Benny.

"Yer wants to 'ear what I knows, I'm sartin."

"Well! what is it?" said Benny, carelessly.

"Your Nelly's killed!"

"It's a lie!" said Benny, paling to the lips.

"'T ain't a lie, neither; she's been run over with a 'bus, an' 'ad her yed cut off."

"You lying thief!" said Benny. "If yer not out o' my sight in a minit I'll pound yer to a jelly."

And Benny made a rush towards him. But Perks was not to be caught, and was soon out of sight.

Benny did not believe a word Perks had said; and yet, somehow, his words troubled him, and very long seemed the time till four o'clock, when he would meet her in the shadow of St. George's Church.

If Perks' only object was to plague and annoy Benny, he could not have been more successful, for try as he would, he could not get Perks' words out of his head. Punctually at four o'clock he was standing by the church, but Nelly was not there, and a dull pain crept into his heart, such as he had never felt before. Five minutes pass – ten minutes – fifteen minutes pass, and still Nelly had not come, and Benny began to fear that something had really happened to her.

Just then he saw Bill Tucker – a boy of his acquaintance – coming towards him.

"Have yer seen Nelly, Bill?" he shouted, when the lad got within hearing distance.

"Ay; ain't yer heerd?"

"Heerd what?" said Benny, growing paler than ever.

"Why, she's got hurt," said the other.

"Are 'e sure, now?" said Benny, great tears starting in his eyes.

"Ay, quite sure. I seed the perlice myself takin' her to the 'firmary."

"Oh, no! 't ain't true, are it, Bill? Say yer afoolin' me,"

said Benny, trembling from head to foot.

"I wish it weren't true," said the lad, "but I seed 'em pick her up mysel', an' I's 'feared she's dead; she looked like it."

"Did a 'bus run over her?"

"No. A big dog runned agin her, an' she fell with her yed on a sharp stone."

"Yer quite sure, Bill?"

"Ay, quite," said the lad; "but go to the 'firmary an' see for yoursel'."

"Which way?" said Benny.

"Haaf-way up Brownlow Hill, an' roun' to the left a mighty big 'ouse."

And off Benny started, like the wind. By dint of many inquiries he found himself in the right street, but looking in vain for the Infirmary.

Just then a policeman came up.

"Could yer tell me where the 'firmary are, please?" said Benny, doffing his cap.

"Why, there, right afore your eyes."

"What, that?" said Benny, pointing to the huge building.

"Ay, to be sure," said the policeman.

"Oh, lor!" was the reply, "I thought that wur the 'ouse the Queen lived in."

The policeman was about to laugh, but noticing Benny's troubled face, he said, "Do you want to get in?"

"Ay," said Benny, "that I do."

"Then go up this street. There's the lodge door on your left; you can't miss it."

"Thanks, sir," and off Benny started. In response to his timid knock the door was opened by a kind-looking man.

"This are the 'firmary, ain't it?" said Benny. "Yes, my little man," was the answer. What do you want?"

"I wants to know if Nelly are in 'ere?"

86

"I don't know. Who is she?"

"My sister," said Benny, the tears starting in his eyes.

"When was she brought here?"

"To-day. Bill Tucker said as 'ow she was hurt in the street an' brought here."

"Yes, a little girl was brought in two or three hours ago."

"Wur she very white, an' had long hair?"

"Yes, my little man."

"Oh, that wur Nelly. Let me see her, please."

"You cannot today, it's against rules; you can see her tomorrow morning, after ten o'clock."

"Oh, do let me jist peep at her."

"I cannot, my little fellow; and besides, it would do her no good."

"But it ud do me good," said Benny, gulping down a great lump in his throat. "She is all I has in the world."

"I'm very sorry, my boy, but you can't see her tonight."

"Not for jist a minit?"

"No, not tonight."

"She ain't dead, then?"

"No, but she is unconscious."

"Will she get better?"

"I hope so. Now run away and come again tomorrow, and rest satisfied that your little sister will be well taken care of."

"Oh, please," said Benny, making a last appeal, the great tears running down his cheeks the while.

"I cannot let you see her, however willing I might be," said the man. "Now run away, there's a good lad."

"Oh, dear," groaned Benny, as he stepped out into the darkening street. "What shall I do? What shall I do?"

He had tasted no food since noon, but he never thought of hunger. He had been on the tramp all the day, but he felt no weariness. There was one great pain in his heart, and that banished every other feeling. Nelly was in that great house suffering, perhaps dying; and he could not speak to her – not even look at her. What right had these people to keep his Nelly from him? Was not she his own little Nell, all that he had in the wide, wide world? How dared they, then, to turn him away?

Hour after hour he wandered up and down in front of the huge building, watching the twinkling lights in its many windows. How could he go away while Nelly was suffering there? Could he sleep in his snug corner while his own little Nell was suffering amongst strangers? It could not be.

So when the great town grew silent around him, he sat down on a doorstep nearly opposite the entrance, and waited for the morning.

The night was chilly, but he felt not the cold; his heart felt as if it would burn through his body. How long the night seemed, and he almost wondered if morning would ever come.

Suddenly a thought struck him. Had he not better pray? He remembered how Nelly prayed every night ere she lay down to sleep, and once he had prayed and felt all the better for it. He would pray again.

So he got up and knelt on the cold flags, and looking up into the silent heavens, where the pale stars kept watch over the sleeping earth, he said, "Oh, Mr. God, I's in great trouble, for Nelly's got hurt, and they's took her into the 'firmary, an' won't let me see her till to-morrer, but You knows all about it, I specks, for Joe says as how You knows everything. But I dunna want her to die, for Joe says You takes people who dies that is good to a mighty nice place; nicer 'n Eastham by a long chalk, an' how You has lots an' lots o' childer; an' if that be the case, I's sure You needn't take little Nell; for oh, Sir, she's all I's got in the world.

Please let her stay an' get better. Oh, do now! for I'll break my heart if she dies. An' 'member, I's only a little chap, an' I's no one but Nelly; an' 'tis so lonesome out here, an' she is there. Please make her better. If I was in Your place, an' You was a little chap like me, I'd let Your Nelly stay. I would for sure. An' oh, if You'll let my Nelly stay an' get better, I'll be awful good. Amen."

Benny waited for a few minutes longer in silence, then got up and crept to the doorstep, and in five minutes after he was fast asleep.

He was aroused in the morning about nine o'clock by the door being opened suddenly, against which he was leaning, and he fell into the passage. He got up as quickly as possible, but not in time to escape a fierce kick dealt him by a hard-featured woman.

Poor child! it was a painful awaking for him. But he was thankful it was broad day. He was cold, and almost faint for want of food, yet he was not conscious of hunger.

When at length he was admitted into the Infirmary he walked as one in a dream. At any other time he would have noticed the long corridors and broad flights of stairs. But he saw nothing of this today. He kept his eyes fixed on the nurse who walked before him, and who was leading him to his little Nell.

He was told that he must be very quiet, and on no account excite her, or it might prove fatal to her, as she was in a very critical state. She had recovered consciousness on the previous night, but she was so weak, and her nervous system had received such a shock, that she could not bear any excitement.

Benny only partly understood what it all meant, but he had determined that he would be very quiet, and make no more noise than he could possibly help. So he followed the pleasant-faced nurse as silently as possible into the Children's Ward. He noticed the two long rows of beds between which they were passing, but he had no eyes for the occupants.

At length the nurse stopped by the side of a little cot, and with a sudden bound he stood by her side. He could hardly repress a cry that rose to his lips, and a great lump rose in his throat that almost choked him; but with a tremendous effort he gulped it down, and brushed away the tears that almost blinded him.

There in the cot was his little Nell, pale as the pillow on which she lay, yet with a look of deep content upon her face, and just the shadow of a smile lingering round the corners of her mouth.

Benny was about to throw his arms around her, but the nurse held up her finger. Nelly's eyes were closed, so that she did not know of their presence, and Benny was made to understand that he must wait until she should open her eyes of her own accord.

So he stood as motionless as the little figure on the bed, gazing with hungry eyes at his little sister, who was silently slipping away from his grasp. He had not to wait long. Slowly the great round eyes opened, the vanishing smile came back and brightened all her face, the lips parted sufficiently for her to whisper "My Benny." And with a low cry Benny bent down his head, and the little wasted arms were twined about his neck, and then the round eyes closed again, and the nurse saw two tears steal out underneath the long lashes, and roll silently down her cheek.

For a few moments they remained thus in silence, then Benny, unable longer to restrain his feelings, sobbed out –

"Oh, Nelly! I can't bear it; my heart's breaking."

"Don't give way so," she said softly. "It's so comfortable

here, an' the good Lord'll take care o' you, Benny."

"But you will soon be better, Nelly, won't you?"

"Yes, Benny, I'll soon be better, but not as you mean it. I's going to Jesus, and shall never have no more cough, nor feel no more pain."

"Oh, no! you's going to get better. I axed the Lord last night to make you better an' let you stay."

"No, Benny, I shan't stay long, I's known it for months, an' I's willin' to go, 'cause I know as how the Lord will take care of you."

"But I canna let you go," said Benny, sobbing louder than ever.

Then the nurse came forward, and laid her hand upon his shoulder. "You must not excite your sister," she said kindly, "for that is not the way to make her better."

"Oh, but she's all l has," he sobbed.

"Yes, poor boy, I know," she replied. "But if your sister leaves you she'll be better off, and will not have to tramp the streets in the cold and wet; so you must think that what is your loss will be her gain."

Nelly raised her eyes to the nurse with a grateful look for talking to Benny in that way. And before he left he had grown calm, and seemingly resigned. It was a painful parting; but Nelly did her best to cheer him up, reminding him that in two days he would be able to come and see her again.

Granny was in great trouble at the absence of the children, and it was no small relief to her when, about noon, Benny put in an appearance at Tempest Court. One look at his face, however, was sufficient to convince her that something had happened, and when Benny told her what had befallen his little Nell, the old woman sat down and cried; for she knew very well that never more would the little face brighten the dingy court. And granny had got to love the sweet, patient little child as her own; and though for months she had been convinced that the little flower was marked to fall, yet it had come in a way she had not expected, and, like Benny, she felt it very hard to give her up.

After dinner Benny went out again to face the world. It was with a very sad heart that he did it; for he felt that from henceforth he would have to fight the battle of life alone.

CHAPTER XII

Fading Away

The morning flowers displayed their sweets,
And gay their silken leaves unfold,
As careless of the noontide heats,
As fearless of the evening cold.

Nipt by the winds' unkindly blast,
Parched by the sun's directer ray,
The momentary glories waste,
The short-lived beauties die away.

S Wesley

JOE Wrag heard the news in silence. Benny, who had gone to him to tell him what had happened to Nell, was not half pleased that he said nothing in reply. But Joe was too troubled to talk. Like granny, he had known for months what was coming, but it had come suddenly, and in a way that he had not expected, and the old man, as he afterwards expressed it, was "struck all of a heap"

Benny waited for some time, but finding Joe was not inclined to talk, he made his way home, leaving the old man gazing into the fire, with a vacant look in his eyes and a look of pain upon his face.

No one ever knew what the old man suffered that night. It was like tearing open the wound that had been made twenty years before, when his only son, as the crowning act of his unkindness, ran away from home, and had never since been heard of.

"If I could only believe that there was the smallest hope o' my ever getting to heaven," he muttered, "it 'ud be easier to bear."

And he hid his face in his hands, while great tears dropped between his fingers to the floor.

"Bless her little heart!" he murmured; "she did not believe as how any wur excluded; she allers stuck to that word 'whosoever,' an' sometimes I wur inclined to think as how she wur right. I wonder, now, if she wur? for sartinly it looks the reasonabler."

"Bless me!" he said after a long pause, "I'm getting mortal shaky in my faith; I used to be firm as a rock. I wonder if it are my heart getting righter, or my head getting wrong. But I mun have a few more talks wi' the little hangel afore she goes."

As soon as Joe was liberated from his watch, he made his way direct to the Infirmary, and bitterly was he disappointed when told that he could not be admitted, and that if he wanted to see the child he must come again on the following day.

His heart was yearning for a sight of her face, and another day and night seemed such a long time to wait; but he turned away without a word, and went slowly home.

Evening found him again at his post of duty, and the next morning found him anxious and sad. The night had seemed so very long, and he was burning with impatience to get away.

The men came to work at length, and off he started with all possible speed. The porter at the door knew him again, and he was admitted without a word.

Nelly was expecting him; she knew it was visitors' day,

and she was certain he would come, so she waited with closed eyes, listening for the footfall of her old friend.

She knew without looking up when he stooped beside her, and reached out her wasted hand, and drew down his weather-beaten wrinkled face and kissed him.

For a long time neither of them spoke. Joe felt if he attempted to utter a word it would choke him, for she was far more wasted than he expected to see her, and somehow he felt that that was the last time they would ever meet on earth.

Nelly was the first to break the silence.

"I's so glad you's come, Joe," she said simply.

"Are'e, my honey?" said Joe, with a choking in his throat.

"Ay," she replied; "I wanted to see yer once more. You's been very good to me, Joe, and to Benny, an' I wanted to thank you afore I died."

"I dunna want thanks, honey," he said, sitting down in the one chair by her bedside, and hiding his face in his hands.

"I know yer does not want 'em, Joe; but it does me good, an' I shall tell the Lord when I gets to heaven how good you've been."

Joe could not reply, and Nelly closed her eyes, and whispered again to herself, as she had often done.

> "Seaward fast the tide is gliding,
> Shores in sunlight stretch away."

Then after a while she spoke again, without opening her eyes.

"You'll not be long afore you comes too, will yer, Joe?"

"Perhaps the Lord will let me look at you through the gate," sobbed Joe; "but I'm afeard He won't let sich as me in."

"Oh, yes, Joe," she said, opening her eyes with such a pained look, "Does you think the Lord does not love yer as much as I do? An' won't He be as glad to see yer as I shall?"

"It does look reasonable like, my purty," said Joe; "but, oh, I'm so afeard."

"'Who-so-ever,'" whispered Nelly, and again closed her eyes, while the troubled expression passed away, and the smile that Joe loved to see came back and lit up her pure *spirituelle* face with a wonderful beauty. And as Joe watched the smile lingering about her mouth as if loth to depart, he felt somehow as if that child had been sent of God to teach him the truth, and to lighten the burden of his dreary life by giving him a hope of heaven.

"'Out of the mouths of babes and sucklings,'" he muttered to himself.

"Yes," said the nurse, coming softly to his side, "out of the mouths of babes He perfects praise."

Joe looked up in surprise. "Do you think the bairn is right?" he stammered out.

"I'm sure of it," she replied.

"But what about the elect?" said Joe, in a tone of voice that proclaimed how deeply he was agitated.

"I think the elect are 'whosoeverwill,'" she replied.

"So Nelly thinks," he said, and shook his head sadly, as if such news were too good to be true.

The nurse, besides being a kind motherly woman who dearly loved children, was also a person of strong common sense, and hence she saw Joe's difficulty in a moment.

"You have no children of your own, I suppose?" she said.

"I had a son once," said Joe. "I hope he's still living."

"You do not love him, of course?"

In a moment Joe was on his feet.

"Love him!" said Joe, trembling from head to foot. "I'd lie down an' die for him this blessed moment if it would do him good."

"Ah! he has been a very good son, I expect," said the nurse.

Joe sat down again, and hid his face in his hands. After a while he looked up and said with evident emotion, "No, he was what people would call a bad son – a very bad 'un."

"Then if he were to come home again, you certainly would close the door against him?"

"Close the door agin him! Close the door agin my own child, my own flesh and blood! Why, I've been longing for years for him to come home. I wish he'd try me, he should have the best of everything I've got in the house. Oh, marcy! how my poor old heart 'ud ache with joy if he were to come tonight."

Joe had got quite excited while delivering himself of this long speech. So the nurse said quietly, "So you think, Joe, that you are better than God."

"Better 'n God?"

"Yes; more merciful, and loving, and kind."

"Who said so?" said Joe, staring at her as if he could scarcely believe his own ears.

"Well, you implied it," said the nurse, quietly. "Me implied it?" said he in a tone of bewilderment. "How so?"

"Well, you say you had a bad son who has been away many years, and yet you say you love him still, so much so that you would willingly die for him; and that, bad as he has been, if he were to come home tonight, instead of driving him from the door, you would give him the heartiest welcome, and think nothing in the house too good for him. And yet you think God will turn away you. So you must admit, Joe," she said with a smile, "that you think you have more love and mercy in your heart than God has in His?"

Joe was silent. And Nelly whispered to the nurse, "Thank you *so* much."

After a while Joe got up, and leaning over the crib, he kissed the pale brow of the little sufferer. "Good bye, my purty," he whispered. "We'll meet again, I do believe."

"Ay, Joe, I'm sure we shall."

"I'm main sorry to lose 'e," he said in a faltering voice, and brushing his rough hand across his eyes; "but I ken give yer to God."

"I'll be waiting, Joe, 'gin you come. Now kiss me, for I'll be gone, I reckon, afore you come again."

Silently Joe bent over her, and pressed a last lingering kiss upon her paling lips. Then sobbing, turned away and left the room.

Granny and Benny called a little later in the day, and found her sinking fast. Her last words to her brother were: "Be good, Benny, an' the Lord will provide, an' we'll meet in heaven." Then she lay as if asleep, taking no further notice of anyone.

Once or twice the nurse heard her repeating, "Seaward fast the tide is gliding," and felt that the words were sadly true.

The nurse told granny that the child was dying, not of the blow on the head, but of swift decline. Nothing could save her, she said. The shock to her nervous system had of course hastened the end; but for that she might have lived till another spring, but certainly not longer. She did not seem to suffer in the least. Hour after hour she lay quite still, while the tide of her little life ebbed swiftly out, and the darkness stole on apace; but she did not fear the gloom. The brave little heart that had borne so patiently the frowns of an unkindly world, was now resting in the love of God.

The smile that had so long flickered over her face like firelight on a wall, now settled into a look of deep content. No murmur ever escaped her lips, not even a sigh; now and then her lips moved as if in prayer, that was all.

And thus she lay waiting for the messenger that should still the little heart into an everlasting rest, and listening for the footfalls that should tell of the coming of her Lord.

After her last look at Benny, she was never seen to open her eyes again, but gradually sank to rest.

> So fades a summer's cloud away,
> So sinks the gale when storms are o'er,
> So gently shuts the eye of day,
> So dies a wave along the shore.

Two days after, Joe and Benny went together to the Infirmary. But they were too late: the pure spirit had gone to God, and the little tired feet were for ever at rest.

"Cannot we see her?" said Benny.

"No, you had better not," was the reply.

Benny felt it very keenly that he might not see his little dead sister, and yet it was best.

They were told, however, if they would be at the New Cemetery at the east of the town on the following day, they might see her buried, and mark her grave.

It was a cold cheerless afternoon when little Nelly Bates was laid in her grave. There was no pomp or display about that funeral, for she was buried at the public expense. Only two mourners stood by the grave, Benny and Joe, but they were mourners indeed.

Benny went from the grave-side of little Nell to his corner under granny's stairs, and sobbed himself to sleep. And Joe went to his hut to muse on the mercy of God, and to revel in his new-found hope of heaven.

CHAPTER XIII

The Tide Turns

Be what thou seemest; live thy creed,
Hold up to earth the torch divine;
Be what thou prayest to be made;
Let the great Master's steps be thine.

Bonar

HOW Benny lived through the next few weeks he never knew. It seemed to him as if the world had become suddenly dark. The one little being who had been the sunshine of his life was buried up in the damp cold grave, and now there seemed nothing to live for, nothing to work for, nothing even to hope for; for what was all the world to him now his little Nell was gone?

He missed her everywhere, and was continually fancying he saw her running to meet him as he drew near the church where they had regularly met for so long a time; and sometimes he would turn round with a sudden start, and with the word "Nelly" on his lips, as he fancied he heard the pattering of her little feet behind him.

He grew despondent, too. While Nelly lived there was someone to work for, someone to bear rebuffs and insults for; but now what did it matter whether he sold his matches or not? He could go hungry; he did not mind. In fact, he did not seem to care what became of him. There seemed to him nothing to fight the world for – nothing.

But for Joe he would have moped his life away in some dark corner where no one could see him. But Joe taught him to believe that his little sister was not lost, only gone before, and that perhaps she looked down upon him from heaven, and that it might grieve her to see him fretting so.

So he tried to sell his matches or earn a penny in some other way in a listless, hopeless manner. But it was very hard work. And when evening came he would drag himself wearily to his little corner under granny's stairs, and generally sob himself to sleep. He missed his little companion in the evenings almost more than at any time, and wished that he had died with her.

Sometimes he went out to the cemetery to see her grave; and no one knew what the little fellow suffered as he knelt there with clasped hands, dropping scalding tears upon the cold earth that hid his little sister from his sight.

He seemed to take no comfort in anything, not even in the story-books that granny had hunted up for him, and which he was beginning to read so nicely. He was proud of his learning while Nelly lived; but all that was changed now.

And so the weeks wore away, and winter came in dark and cold. But people generally did not seem to mind the darkness nor the cold, for Christmas was drawing near, and they were anticipating a time of mirth and merrymaking, of friendly greetings and family gatherings.

The trains began to be crowded again with homecomers for their holidays; shopkeepers began to vie with each other as to which could present in their windows the grandest display; the streets were crowded with well-dressed people who were getting in a stock of Christmas cheer; and everywhere people seemed bent on enjoying themselves to the utmost of their ability.

All this, however, only seemed to make Benny sadder than ever. He remembered how the Christmas before Nelly was with him, and he was as happy and light-hearted as he well could be. Yet now the very happiness of the people seemed to mock his sorrow, and he wished that Christmas was gone again.

One bitterly cold afternoon he was at his old place, waiting for the railway boat to come up to the stage, in the hope that some one of its many passengers would permit him to carry his or her bag, when he noticed a gentleman standing against the side of the boat with a portmanteau in his right hand, and holding the hand of a little girl with his left.

The boat was a long time coming to, for a heavy sea was running at the time, and the gentleman seemed to get terribly impatient at the delay. But Benny was rather glad of it, for he had abundant opportunity of looking at the little girl, whose pleasant, smiling face reminded him more of his little dead sister than any face he had ever seen.

"Golly, ain't she purty!" said Benny to himself; "and don't that woolly stuff look hot round her jacket! And what long hair she have! – a'most as long as little Nell's," and he brushed his hand quickly across his eyes. "An' she looks good an' kind, too. I specks the gent is her par."

And Benny regarded the gentleman more attentively than he had hitherto done.

"Well, now, ain't that cur'us!" he muttered. "If that ain't the very gent whose portmantle I carried the night father wolloped me so. I'll try my luck agin, for he's a good fare, an' not to be sneezed at."

By this time the gangway had been let down, and the gentleman and his little girl were among the first to hurry on to the stage. In a moment Benny had stepped forward, and touching his cap very respectfully, said, "Carry yer bag, sir?

"No," said the gentleman shortly, and hurried on.

"Oh, please, sir, do!" said Benny, his eyes filling with tears. "I's had no luck today."

But the gentleman did not heed his tears or his pleading voice. He had been annoyed at the delay of the boat, and he was in no mood to brook further delay. So he said sternly, "Be off with you this moment!"

Benny turned away with a great sob, for since Nelly died rebuffs had become doubly hard to bear. He did not try to get another fare, but stood looking out on the storm-tossed river, trying to gulp down the great lumps that rose continually in his throat.

"I specks I'll have to starve," he thought bitterly, "for I can't get a copper today nohow."

Just then he felt a touch on his arm, and turning his brimming eyes, he saw the little girl he had noticed on the boat.

"What's the matter, little boy?" she said, in a voice that sounded like music to the sad-hearted child.

They were the first kind words that had been spoken to him for the day, and they completely broke him down.

At length he stammered out between his sobs, "Oh, I's so hungry an' cold, an' little Nelly's dead; an' all the world is agin me."

"Have you no father?" she said.

"No; I's no father, nor mother, nor sister, nor nobody. Nelly was all I had in the world, an' now she's dead."

"Poor boy!" said the kindly little voice. "And how do you get your living?"

"Oh, I sells matches or carries gents' portmantles when they'll let me, or anything honest as turns up."

"Well, don't think papa is unkind because he spoke cross to you, but he had been annoyed. And here is a shilling he gave me today; you need it more than I do, so I will give it to you. Are you here every day?"

"Ay, I's mostly here every day," said Benny, closing his fingers around the bright shilling as one in a dream.

The next moment he was alone. He looked everywhere for the little girl, but she was nowhere visible.

"Golly!" said Benny, rubbing his eyes, "I wonder now if she wur a hangel. Nelly said as 'ow the Lord 'ud provide. An' mebbe He sent her with that bob. I wish I had looked more particler to see if she had wings, 'cause Nelly said as how hangels had wings."

More than twenty times that afternoon Benny looked at the bright new shilling that had been given him; the very sight of it seemed to do him good. It seemed to turn the tide, too, in his favour, for before dark he had earned another shilling; and that evening he trudged to his home with a lighter heart than he had known for many a week.

The weather on Christmas Eve was anything but orthodox. There was neither frost nor snow; but, on the contrary, it was close and sultry. Benny had been out in the neighbourhood of Edge Hill with a big bundle for a woman, who dismissed him with three halfpence, and the remark that young vagabonds like he always charged twice as much as they expected to get. So Benny was trudging home in a not very happy frame of mind. He had been tolerably fortunate, however, during the early part of the day, and that compensated him to some extent for his bad afternoon's work.

As he was passing along a street in the neighbourhood of Falkner Square he was arrested by the sound of music and singing. Now, as we have hinted before, Benny was very sensitive to the influence of music, and, in fact, anything beautiful had a peculiar charm for him. The window of the

104

house before which he stopped stood slightly open, so that he was, not only able to hear the music, but also to distinguish the words that were being sung.

It was a pure childish voice that was singing to a simple accompaniment on the piano –

> "There is beauty all around,
> When there's love at home;
> There is joy in every sound,
> When there's love at home.
> Peace and plenty here abide,
> Smiling sweet on every side;
> Time doth softly, sweetly glide,
> When there's love at home."

Benny waited, as if rooted to the ground, until the song ended; waited a minute longer in the hope that the singer would begin again. And in that minute the little singer came to the window and looked out and saw our hero; and Benny, looking up at the same moment, saw the face of his angel, and hurried away out of sight, as if he had been guilty of some wrong.

The little singer was Eva Lawrence, the daughter of a well-to-do man of business in the town. She was not ten years of age by several months, but she was unusually thoughtful for her age, and was as kind-hearted as she was thoughtful.

As soon as Mr. Lawrence had finished his tea that evening, and had betaken himself to his easy chair, little Eva clambered upon his knee, and, putting her arms about his neck, said, "Papa, what do you think?"

"Oh, I think ever so many things," he replied, laughing.

"Now, you naughty man, you're going to tease again. But I've begun wrong way about, as usual. I want to ask a favour."

"I expected as much, Eva," said her father, smiling. "But

how many more Christmas presents will you want?"

"But this is not a present exactly."

"Oh, indeed," he said, pretending to look serious.

"Now, don't be a tease," she said, pulling his whiskers, "for I'm quite serious. Now listen."

"I'm all attention, my dear."

"You want a little boy to run errands and sweep out the office, and do little odd jobs, don't you?"

"Well, who has been telling you that?"

"Nobody, papa; I only wanted to know, you see. So you do, don't you?"

"Well, I shall the beginning of the year, for the boy I have is leaving. But what has that to do with my little girl?"

"Well, papa, our teacher is always telling us that we ought to be little missionaries, and lend a helping hand to the needy whenever possible, and do all the good we can."

"Quite right, my dear; but I can't see yet what my little girl is driving at."

"Well, she was telling us only last Sunday that lots of people would be better if they had better surroundings; and that if something could be done to get those little street Arabs more out of the reach of temptation, they might grow up to be good and honest men and women."

"Well, Eva?"

"Well, papa, I should like for you to give one of those little street boys a chance."

"Who do you mean?"

"That poor boy I gave the shilling to on the landing-stage the other day, don't you remember – when you called me a silly girl?"

"And were you not silly, Eva?"

"No, papa, I don't think I was; for I am sure the boy is not bad, he has such honest eyes. And he said he had no father, nor mother, nor brother, nor sister, and he seemed in such trouble."

"Well, my child?"

"You know now what I mean, papa. I confess I had quite forgotten the poor boy till this afternoon I saw him standing in front of the house. I had been singing 'Love at Home,' and he had been listening, I think; and I fancy it had made him sad, for his eyes were full of tears, but when he saw he was noticed he hurried away as quickly as possible."

"And suppose I should decide to employ this boy, Eva, where should I find him?"

"Oh, he said he was nearly always on the landing-stage. He sold matches there, except when he was running errands."

"Well, I will think about it, Eva."

"Oh, promise, papa, there's a good man."

"I don't believe in making rash promises, Eva," said Mr. Lawrence kindly; "and, besides, I have very little faith in those street boys. They are taught to be dishonest from their infancy, and it is a difficult matter for them to be anything else; but I'll think about it."

And Mr. Lawrence was as good as his word; he did think about it, and, what is more, he decided to give the little boy a trial.

Benny was on the landing-stage on New Year's Day when Mr. Lawrence was returning from Chester. He had scarcely left the railway boat when several lads crowded around him with "Carry yer bag, sir?" Benny among the number.

He quickly recognised our hero from the description Eva gave, and placed his bag in Benny's hand, giving him the address of his office. Arrived there, much to Benny's bewilderment, he was invited inside, and Mr. Lawrence began to ply him with questions, all of which he answered in a straightforward manner, for there was little in his life that he cared to hide.

Mr. Lawrence was so much impressed in the boy's favour that he engaged him at once, promising him two shillings a week more than he had intended to give.

When Benny at length comprehended his good fortune – for it was some time before he did – he sobbed outright. Looking up at length with streaming eyes, he blurted out, "I can't tell 'e how 'bliged I is," and ran out of the office and hurried home to tell granny the news, not quite certain in his own mind whether he was awake or dreaming.

Granny was upstairs when Benny burst into the room, and when she came down the first thing she saw was Benny standing on his head.

"Oh, granny," he shouted, "I's made my fortin! I's a gent at last!"

Granny was a considerable time before she could really discover from Benny what had happened; but when she did discover she seemed as pleased as the child. And a bigger fire was made up, and a more sumptuous supper was got ready in honour of the occasion.

CHAPTER XIV

A Glimpse of Paradise

I know not how others saw her,
But to me she was wholly fair;
And the light of the heaven she came from
Still lingered and gleamed in her hair;

For it was as wavy and golden,
And as many changes took,
As the shadow of sunlight ripples
On the yellow bed of a brook.

J.R. Lowell

FOR the next month Benny lived in a seventh heaven of delight. The only drawback to his happiness was that Nelly was not alive to share his good fortune. Time was mercifully blunting the keen edge of his sorrow, and day by day he was getting more reconciled to his loss. Yet never a day passed but that he wished a hundred times that his little sister were still with him, that they might rejoice together in his good fortune. He knew that she was better off, and even hoped that she was not altogether ignorant of his success in life. Yet how much pleasanter it would have been, he thought, if they could have journeyed on through life together.

Benny had wonderful dreams of future success. Though not of a very imaginative: temperament, he could not help occasionally indulging in daydreams and castle-building, and some of his castles, it must be admitted, were of a most magnificent description.

He saw the glowing heights before him, the summits of which others had reached, and why might not he? He certainly had commenced the ascent: what was there to hinder him from reaching the top? Had not granny told him of poor Liverpool boys who, by perseverance and honest toil, had be-come wealthy men, and were now occupying high and honourable positions? Surely, then, there was a chance for him, and if he did not succeed it should not be for want of trying.

He felt that already he had got his foot on the first rung of the ladder, and if there was any chance of his reaching the top he would do it. And as he thought thus, the future opened out before him in glowing vistas of unimagined beauty.

He knew that he must wait many years that he must work hard and patiently; that perhaps many difficulties would arise that he could not foresee; still, still, across the boggy valley the mountain rose up with its sunlighted crown, and the question came back – Others had reached the top, then why might not he?

It is true he never attempted to put these thoughts into words. They seemed to him too big for utterance; yet they were always with him, lightening his toil and brightening the long future that lay before him.

If Benny had been of a less practical turn of mind, he might have done what so many others have done – dreamed his life away, or waited idly for fortune to drop her treasures in his lap. But Benny, notwithstanding his occasional daydreams, was sufficiently matter-of-fact to know that if he was to win any success in life, it must be by hard work.

He was already able to read very creditably. But now a

new desire seized him – he would learn to write as well. But how was he to begin? He had to confess that that was a poser, for neither granny nor Joe could give him any assistance. Still he had set his heart upon learning to write, and he was not to be defeated.

So one day he said to one of Mr. Lawrence's clerks, "Does yer think, Mr. Morgan, that I could learn to write if I was to try very hard?"

"Of course you could, Benny," said Mr. Morgan, looking kindly down into the dark earnest-looking eyes of the office boy. For Benny had done several little things for Mr. Morgan, and so that gentleman was disposed to be kind to the little waif.

"But how is I to begin?" said Benny eagerly.

"I'm busy now," said Mr. Morgan, "but if you will wait till tomorrow, I'll bring you a slate and pencil and will set you a copy, and then you'll be able to begin right off."

Just then Mr. Lawrence called Benny from the inner office, and sent him with a note to Mrs. Lawrence, with instructions to wait for an answer.

"You know the way, Benny"

"Yes, sir."

"But you've never been to the house?"

"No, sir."

"Then how do you know the way?"

"It's where you has the music an' 'love at home' sir, ain't it?"

Mr. Lawrence smiled and said, "You are on the right track, Benny, I think. Go to the house, and give this note to the servant that opens the door, and say that you have to wait for an answer."

"Yes, sir," said Benny, bowing very politely, and hurrying out of the office.

Benny had often longed to listen under the window of

Mr. Lawrence's house that he might hear again the song that had so touched his heart, and see again the little angel face through whose intercession he owed his good fortune; for Mr. Lawrence had hinted as much as that to him. But even if nothing had ever been said, he would still have connected Mr. Lawrence's kindness to him with his little daughter, who had spoken so kindly to him in the hour of his sorrow and despair, and whose bright shilling he still kept, and regarded with almost superstitious reverence.

But he had never dared to listen under the window again; he felt somehow as if he had no business in that neighbourhood, no right to look upon the face of his little benefactress; so he kept away and spent his long winter evenings by granny's fireside, poring over the few books that she and Joe were able to procure for him.

Benny could not help wondering, as he hurried along the streets, holding the letter very carefully in his hand, whether he would see again the little face at the window or hear her voice in song. He hoped that one or the other would greet him; but he was disappointed in both. No face was at the window, no sound of music floated out on the bright frosty air.

He pulled the door-bell very timidly, and then waited a long time very patiently for the door to open. It was opened, however, at length, and, bowing very low, he said, "Please,'m, here's a letter from the master, an' I's to wait for an answer."

"You'll have to wait some time, then," said the girl, scornfully, "for Mrs. Lawrence has gone out; but come inside," and she shut the door with a bang.

"May I wait here?" said Benny, looking round the roomy hall.

"Yes," said the girl. "I'll have no brats in the kitchen; you can sit on that chair if you like;" and she hurried downstairs.

Benny obeyed, and sat for a long time holding his cap between his knees. At length, as he was growing rather impatient, he heard a light step on the stairs near him, and, looking up, he saw his little benefactress descending, carrying a huge doll in her arms.

Benny felt himself growing hot all over, for he had no idea whether it was the proper thing to stand or sit still, so he shuffled about on his chair in a very uneasy manner.

The little girl looked at him curiously for a moment, and then came towards him, saying, "Are you not Benny, that papa has in his office?"

"Yes, 'm," said Benny, shuffling dangerously near the edge of the chair, and blushing to the roots of his hair.

"Don't be frightened," she said, noticing his embarrassment. "I've been wanting a long time to see you. Are you waiting for something?"

"Ay," said Benny regaining his composure; "the master sent me with a letter, an' told me to wait an answer."

"Well, mamma won't be in yet, so you can come into the nursery; it is warm there."

Benny had not the remotest idea what a nursery was, but he followed his guide at what he thought a very respectful distance, and soon found himself in the most wonderful room he had ever seen in his life. Toys of every description were scattered about, and pictures of every description adorned the walls. A swing was suspended from the ceiling in the centre of the room, and in the nearest corner was a doll's house furnished in magnificent style. But what most attracted Benny's attention was a huge rocking-horse. At first he thought it was alive, but soon found out his mistake, though his wonderment was not in the least diminished by his discovery.

113

Little Eva Lawrence was evidently amused at Benny's astonishment, and after regarding him for some time with a merry twinkle in her eyes, said, "Did you never see a rocking-horse before, Benny?"

"Never!" was the laconic reply.

"Would you like to ride, Benny?"

"Wouldn't I just!" said Benny, his eyes beaming with pleasure.

"Well, here are the steps; take care you don't fall off, though," said Eva.

"Oh, never fear," said Benny, mounting the horse. "Now for 't, miss, an' see if I ain't a stunner at it!"

And the next moment our hero was sprawling on the floor in the middle of the room.

"Golly!" he ejaculated, picking himself up with a bewildered air, and scratching his head. "I's floored, to a sartinty."

"You tried to go too fast to begin with," laughed Eva; "you'll do better next time."

"May I try again?" he questioned.

"Oh, yes," was the reply; "I want you to enjoy yourself."

And enjoy himself he did, to his heart's content.

After a while Eva said, "Now, Benny, I want to know more about you: won't you tell me something about yourself and about your little sister?"

"Ay, that I will, if you wish," said Benny, sitting down in a low chair before the fire. And in his simple childish way he told her all the story with which the reader is acquainted – for he had lost all shyness now – told it with a simple eloquence and pathos that brought the tears again and again to his little listener's eyes. Ay, he wept himself when he told of his little sister, of her goodness and of her love. He did not even hide from his listener the story of his temptation, and how but for his little Nelly he would have been a thief in act as well as in heart.

With the account of little Nelly's death Eva was much affected, and Benny sobbed again as the recollection of his loss came back to him.

"I thought I should ha' died when she were took," said he, between his sobs.

"Poor little boy!" said Eva, soothingly; "but you see your little sister's words have come true, after all."

"What words, Miss?"

"Why, what you told me just now, Benny – how the Lord would provide."

"Oh, ay," said Benny, reflectively, "though I wur as near as nothin' to starvin' the day I fust seed you."

"Were you? Then perhaps the Lord sent me to help you."

"Oh, no doubt on that score," said Benny, stoutly; "I's sartin about that matter."

"Do you go to Sunday-school, Benny?" Benny shook his head.

"Nor to church or chapel?"

"Not since that night me an' Nelly went, that I told you 'bout."

"How is that?"

"Well, we did try to get into another place o' the sort, smarter like, but the gent at the door shoved us out, an' said there wur no room for such brats as us, an' told us to be off 'bout our bizness."

"Poor boy! said Eva, wondering if he came to the chapel she attended if he would not receive similar treatment.

At length she looked up and said, "I would go to that chapel again, that you and Nelly attended, if I were you, on a Sunday. It would not be closed then, and I'm sure that kind gentleman would be glad to have you in the Sunday-school."

"Oh, then, I'll go," said Benny, who felt that this little girl's wish was law to him.

Soon after Mrs. Lawrence came in, read her husband's note without a word, and hastily wrote a reply.

"Make haste, Benny," she said kindly, giving him the letter she had written. "I'm afraid Mr. Lawrence will think you've been away a very long time."

Benny took the letter without a word, and hurried away with a heart full of gratitude for the kindly treatment he had received. It seemed to him as if that day he had had a glimpse of Paradise, and had spoken to one of God's angels face to face.

How bright and smooth his path of life was growing! He almost feared sometimes that he was dreaming, and that he would awake and find himself destitute and forsaken.

He was now beginning to enjoy life, and as he looked back upon the past he almost wondered how he and his little sister had managed to live in those dark years of cold and want.

When Joe Wrag first heard of Benny's good fortune he lifted up his hands, and said in a voice of reverence, "The Lord is good! the Lord is good!" Then after a moment's pause he went on, "But oh! what an old sinner I've a-been, to be sure!"

"How so?" said Benny.

"How so? 'cause as how I turned my back upon God, an' tried to persuade mysel' that He had turned His back on me. Oh, I did, lad, an' in my heart I called Him 'ard names. I didn't dare say it wi' my lips, but in my heart, boy, I said He wur cruel – that He wur a monster, that He had no feelin', that He had shut the door agin' me, when all the time He – wur a-sayin', "Joe, come back, come back, for there's room in the Father's heart and home for thee." But, oh! praise His name, He sent His hangel to tell poor owd Joe the way, an' reveal the Father's love – He did, boy, for sure."

"His hangel, Joe?" said Benny, trying in vain to comprehend all Joe had said.

"Ay, His hangel, boy. An' that angel wur little Nell, bless her! she's wi' Him now, in the land where there's no more sorrow nor pain, an' Joe's on the way."

And the old man looked up into the star-bespangled sky, as if he would look through the very floor of heaven.

Benny thought of all this, as he hurried from Mr. Lawrence's door, and felt as if he, too, had had an angel sent from God to help him on the way to heaven.

Poor boy! he did not see the heavy cloud that was gathering in the sky, nor the dark and painful paths that lay before him, which he, with bruised and bleeding feet, would have to tread. He only saw the promised land, bathed in sunshine and clad in beauty, a land where plenty reigned and want could never come, and knew not of the weary wilderness that lay between. He thought that he had passed through the wilderness already, and that all the sorrow, and hunger, and pain lay behind him.

It was well he did so. Let him enjoy the sunshine while it lasts, and dream his happy dreams of coming joy. The awaking will come all too soon. Poor boy! may God protect him in the struggle of life.

CHAPTER XV

A Terrible Alternative

Sow truth, if thou the true wouldst reap,
Who sows the false shall reap the vain;
Erect and sound thy conscience keep,
From hollow words and deeds refrain.

Sow love, and taste its fruitage pure;
Sow peace, and reap its harvest bright;
Sow sunbeams on the rock and moor,
And reap a harvest home of light.

Bonar

THE days of peace and sunshine sped all too swiftly. Winter soon gave place to budding spring, and spring lengthened into summer. Twelve months had passed since that happy day in Eastham Woods, for June had come again; and the parks and squares were once more green, and the streets were hot and dusty.

It had been a strange year to Benny. Pain and pleasure had strangely commingled. Never had he felt such sorrow, never had he known such joy. The old year had closed in sorrow and despair; the new year had opened in joy and hope.

Benny had grown much during those twelve months, for neither the chastening of grief nor the stimulus of kindness had been lost upon him. Both had done him good, and so

118

the year had been to him one of growth – growth in every sense. He had grown physically. He was barely twelve yet, but he was well developed for his age; especially so considering how little had been the care bestowed on his childhood. His face was open and pleasant, and there was a frank honest expression in his eyes that won him favour wherever he went.

He had grown, too, mentally. Mr. Morgan had regularly set him copies, and Mr. Lawrence, discovering his eagerness to learn, had lent him books that would help him in the pursuit of knowledge. He became a most diligent student. At first he sought after knowledge as a means to an end. He believed that it would help him in the race of life. But the farther he advanced the pleasanter became his studies, and knowledge became precious for its own sake. What at first he set before himself as a stern and even unpleasant duty, became at last a joy and delight.

He was eager also to improve his manners. He was anxious to speak correctly, and not be a disgrace to the gentleman who employed him and the butt of the clerks. And it was wonderful what progress he made in this respect. It is true that he frequently forgot himself, and the old expressions that habit had made familiar rolled easily from his tongue. But he had made up his mind to conquer, and he was certainly succeeding.

And last, but not least, he had grown morally. For three months he had regularly attended the Sunday-school, and among the five hundred boys and girls that assembled regularly week after week there was not a more diligent inquirer than Benny. The spiritual discernment that Joe Wrag thought he lacked was being given, and the "old, old story" was beginning to have a wonderful fascination for him.

Mr. Lawrence was wonderfully pleased with his *protégé*,

and had decided that if during the next six months he made such progress as he had done in the past, he should be promoted to a higher position.

Benny regarded his fortune as made. Never had life seemed so bright to him as, one Saturday afternoon, he was busy at work putting Mr. Lawrence's office in order. There was no one in the office but himself. Mr. Lawrence had just left, giving him instructions that he must wait till Mr. Morgan returned, who would lock up the offices, and then he (Benny) must bring up the keys to his residence.

Benny had swept out the inner office, put the few books that were lying about in their proper places on the shelves, and was busy dusting the furniture, humming to himself the song that haunted him continually ...

> "There is beauty all around,
> When there's love at home,"

... when Mr. Lawrence came in hurriedly, and went straight to his desk and began to search carefully among the few papers that were lying on it; then he looked behind it, around it, and underneath it, but it was evident, from the perplexed look on his face, that he could not find what he was in search of.

"Benny," he called, "come here."

And Benny came in from the outer office, to which he had retired on Mr. Lawrence's appearance.

"Has Mr. Morgan returned yet?" demanded Mr. Lawrence, in a stern voice.

"No, sir," said Benny, wondering what had happened.

"Has anyone been here since I left?"

"No, sir."

"You are quite sure?"

"Yes, sir, quite sure."

"Then will you tell me what has become of the five-pound note that I left lying on the desk when I went out?" And he looked straight in Benny's face.

Benny turned pale, for he knew what the question implied, but he did not quail before Mr. Lawrence's stern gaze, and, looking his employer straight in the eyes, he answered, "I do not know, sir; I have not seen it."

"Now, Benny," said Mr. Lawrence, "mind what you are saying."

In a moment his face flushed crimson as he answered, "Did you ever know me lie, sir?"

"No, Benny," answered Mr. Lawrence; "I never did, nor steal either. Though I can quite conceive how, in a moment of weakness, you might be tempted to do both."

"But I've done neither," said Benny, with trembling lip.

For a moment Mr. Lawrence was silent, then he said, "Look here, Benny. I left a five-pound note on the desk when I went out. I am quite certain of that – as certain as I am that I stand here at this moment. And, according to your own statement, no one but yourself has been in the office since I left, and when I come back the note is gone. What am I to think?"

"It's mighty queer, sir," said Benny, turning pale again; "but I hope you'll not think that I've took it."

"I'm afraid that I must think so."

Then there was another pause, while Benny trembled from head to foot. At length Mr. Lawrence spoke again.

"I do not wish to be hard with you, Benny," he said; "and if you will only confess that you have taken the note, I will forgive you."

"And if I was to tell a lie and say I took it, you would ask me for it at once, and I ain't got it." And Benny burst into tears.

"No, I will be more lenient still, for I know what a grief it will be to my little girl when she hears about it. If you will only confess that you have taken it, I won't even ask you to return it. But if you will not confess, I'm afraid the law will have to take its course."

Poor Benny! It was a terrible moment to him, and he tried to realise how much depended upon his answer. By telling a lie he might still keep his situation and the friendship of his little benefactress, and yet reach the heights to which his ambition pointed. But if he stuck to the truth, what would there be? A prison, perhaps, and then the old life in the streets – hunger and weariness and cold. True, if he told a lie Mr. Lawrence would then have no doubt of his guilt. But, alas! he would still believe him guilty if he told the truth, and not only Mr. Lawrence, but every one else that knew him would regard him as a thief.

It was a terrible alternative. Tell a lie, and still go on the shining way that for months had been opening up before him; tell the truth, and go back to the old life, that would now seem worse than death – go back to want and disgrace.

At one time he would not have been long in deciding the question. But conscience had been awakened since then, and, while he hesitated, the little pale face of his dead sister rose up between him and his employer, and a voice within seemed to whisper, "Tell the truth, Benny, and the Lord will provide."

It was a brief interval since Mr. Lawrence had spoken, but in those few moments Benny had fought the fiercest battle of his life, and had won the victory.

He lifted his swimming eyes to Mr. Lawrence and said, "I cannot tell a lie, sir." That was all.

Mr. Lawrence regarded him for a few moments in silence, then left the office with a deeply puzzled expression on his face. He did not know what to think. Either Benny was honest, or he was a most hardened thief, and somehow he felt that the boy could not be the latter. He had always found him so truthful and thoughtful and obliging. There seemed nothing bad about the boy. And yet where could that note be if he had not taken it?

And again he walked back into the office, and commenced a search more careful and diligent than before, but all without avail: the note was nowhere to be found.

Sorely puzzled what to do, he left the office once more, and had scarcely got into the street when he stumbled across Police-inspector Sharp.

"Good afternoon," said the inspector, touching his hat.

"Good afternoon," said Mr. Lawrence, passing on. He had not gone many steps, however, before he turned back.

"I don't know but that it is a fortunate thing, Sharp, that I have met you," he said. "The fact is, I'm in a bit of a difficulty, and I don't know a more likely man than you to help me out."

"I'm at your service, sir," said Mr. Sharp, "and it I can render you any assistance, I shall be most happy to do so."

"Well, the fact is," said Mr. Lawrence, and he went on to tell all the circumstances connected with the missing note, and finished up by saying, "But somehow I cannot for the life of me believe the boy has stolen it."

"Indeed, now," said Mr. Sharp, putting on a professional air, "I cannot for the life of me believe that the urchin has *not* stolen it. So you see my difficulty is in the opposite direction, Mr. Lawrence."

"But you don't know this lad, Mr. Sharp."

"Well, perhaps I don't know this particular young dog, but I know the whole tribe of them," said Mr. Sharp, trying to look wise, "and I tell you they are all rogues and vagabonds, from the oldest to the youngest of 'em. Bless you, it is bred in their very bones, and they couldn't be honest if they were to try ever so."

"But this boy has been with me six months, and a nicer lad I never knew."

"Ay, yes, Mr. Lawrence, their cunning is amazing; and they can play the hypocrite equal to old Satan himself. I tell you what, sir, if you had had the experience of 'em that I've had, you'd mistrust the whole tribe of 'em."

"Well, I dare say, Sharp, you know more about them than I do, and I confess that it was with some amount of misgiving that I engaged the boy; but he has never taken anything before."

"Did you ever give him the chance?"

"Well, perhaps not," said Mr. Lawrence, looking thoughtful.

"Just so," said Inspector Sharp. "The young dog has patiently waited his opportunity. Oh, bless you, sir, they know their game."

"But what had I better do?" said Mr. Lawrence, looking puzzled.

"If you'll leave the matter to me," said Mr. Sharp, "I'll work the oracle for you, and very likely restore you the missing money."

"I'm very unwilling to prosecute," said Mr. Lawrence, in a troubled tone of voice.

"Just so, just so. I quite understand your feeling. But you'll not have need to do much in that direction, I can assure you," said Mr. Sharp, in a patronising manner.

"Well," said Mr. Lawrence, looking like a man that had made up his mind to submit to a painful operation, "I'll leave the matter in your hands."

Half an hour later, as Benny stood in the street waiting

until Mr. Morgan had locked the doors, a police constable came forward and touched him on the arm.

"You'll come with me!" he said. "I've found fresh lodgings for you tonight."

"Did Mr. Lawrence send you?" said Benny, the tears standing in his eyes.

"The orders came from him in the first place," said the policeman; "he intends to stop your cribbing for a week or two."

"Oh, but I didn't steal the money," sobbed Benny, "I didn't really."

"They all say that," laughed the constable; "but from what I can hear, you're a particular cunning dog. However, you're caught this time."

Benny felt that it was of no use saying any more, so he walked along by the officer's side with the calmness of despair settling down upon his heart.

He had no wish to resist. He knew it would be useless for him to attempt to do so. He had lost everything now, and the only thing he hoped for was that death might come speedily, and that he might soon be laid to rest by the side of his little sister, and be at peace for ever.

He thought everybody was looking at him, as the officer led him through the streets, and he could not help feeling thankful now that Nelly was dead. Such disgrace would break her heart if she were alive. And for the first time he felt glad that she was sleeping in her grave.

How changed everything had become in one short day! A few hours ago he was mourning the loss of his sister; now he was glad that she was numbered with the dead. But one short hour before the world had never seemed so bright, and he had thought how he should enjoy the beautiful summer evening in Wavertree Park; now the world had never seemed so cheerless and dark, and his evening was to be spent in a prison cell.

Poor boy! It is no wonder that he wished he might die, for every hope had been blasted in an hour.

On arriving at the police station he was thrust into his cell without a word. He was thankful to find that it was empty, for he wanted to be alone with his thoughts. Selecting the darkest corner, he crouched down upon the floor and rested his head upon his knees. He could not weep, his grief was too great for tears. He could only think and think, until his thoughts seemed to scorch his very brain. And as he crouched thus, while the hours of that summer's afternoon and evening dragged slowly along, his whole life passed vividly before him, he seemed to live it all over again, and he asked himself if he could go back to the old life of hunger and cold in the streets.

When Nelly was with him, and they knew no other life, they were not unhappy. But he had had a glimpse of Paradise since then. He had tasted the joys of hope and had cherished dreams of a happy future, and he felt that it would be easier to die than to return in disgrace to what he had thought he had left behind him for ever.

It was very hard that just as the world seemed brightest, and hope seemed growing into certainty – just as the path of life was getting clear, and the end seemed certain, that he should be thus thrust down, and thrust down to a lower depth than he had known in his darkest days.

Could it be true, he asked himself again and again, that he, who had been trying so hard to be good and truthful and honest, was really in prison on a charge of theft? It had come upon him so suddenly that he thought sometimes it must be all some horrid dream, and that he would surely awake some time and find the bright future still before him.

And so the hours wore away, and the light faded in the little patch of sky that was visible through his high grated window, and the cell grew darker and more dismal all the while.

At length there was a tramp of feet in the courtyard outside. The key grated in the lock, the door flew open, and two lads were tumbled into the cell. These were followed in half an hour by three others, and Benny became aware by the noises in the courtyard that other cells were being filled as well as the one he occupied. And, as the darkness deepened, night grew hideous with shouts, and laughter, and songs, and curses loud and deep.

It seemed to him as if he had got to the very mouth of hell. Nothing that he had ever heard in Addler's Hall or Bowker's Row could at all compare with what he heard that night: now there was the sound of blows; now cries for help; now shrieks of murder, accompanied by volleys of oaths and shouts of laughter.

The companions of his own cell were on the whole tolerably orderly, and were evidently disposed to make the best of their situation. They started several songs, but in every case broke down at the end of the second line, so at length they gave up trying, and settled themselves down to sleep.

It was far on towards morning before all grew still, but silence did drop down upon the prisoners at last; and Benny, weary with counting the beats of his heart, dropped at length into a troubled sleep. It was late in the morning when he awoke again, and for a moment he was unable to recall what had happened or where he was. Then the memory of the past evening rushed in upon him like a flood, and he buried his face in his hands in the misery of despair.

He wondered what granny would think of his absence, and what his teacher would think in the Sunday-school. Alas! he should see them no more, for how could he go to them with such a stain upon his name?

While he was musing thus he was startled by a familiar voice addressing him, and looking up he saw Perks looking at him, with a broad grin upon his countenance.

"Well, this are a onexpected pleasure!" he said. "I's jolly glad to see yer, Ben. Yer see, I's of a very forgivin' natur'."

But Benny made no reply. He only wondered if his misery would ever end.

"In the dumps, eh?" continued Perks. "Well, I an' my mates'll help you out in quick sticks: now let's have a song all together. You ken take the big end, that's the bass, yer know."

"I want to be quiet," said Benny; "do let me alone."

"In course I'll let 'e alone. I looks like it, don't I? I's a very forgivin' natur, Mister Benjamin Bates, you knows that, though I don't forget. But the fact is, I's so pleased to 'ave yer company agin that I'm bound to show my delight in some way."

"If you don't take yourself off, Perks, you'll wish you had," said Benny.

"Now, don't be touchy, Mr. Bates. But let's dance a cornpipe, while one o' my mates whistles Pop goes the Weasel.'"

Poor Benny! he could not escape his tormentor, so he bore throughout that weary Sabbath, as best he could, a series of petty persecutions. He tried to be patient, he even tried to pray, but the only prayer he could utter was, "O Lord, kill me at once, and put me out of misery."

CHAPTER XVI

An Experiment

Sew ye beside all waters,
Where the dew of heaven may fail;
Ye shall reap, if ye be not weary,
For the Spirit breathes o'er all.

Sow, though the thorns may wound thee,
One wore the thorns for thee;
And though the cold world scorn thee,
Patient and hopeful be.

Anna Shipton

WHILE Benny in his prison-cell was dragging out the weary hours of that June Sabbath, Joe Wrag was engaged in an experiment that had occupied his thoughts for some considerable time. Since that never-to-be-forgotten day when he had kissed his little Nelly a last good bye, he had never doubted three things: – First, that the elect were "whosoever will;" second, that he had been accepted of the Father; and, third, that little Nelly Bates had been to him the "sent of God," to lead him out of the darkness of error into the light of truth.

The certainty that he was included in God's invitation of mercy was to him a new revelation. He felt as if he had suddenly grown young again, and, notwithstanding his grief for his little pet, he experienced a joy springing up in his heart the like of which he had never known before.

The words that have comforted so many sorrow-bruised hearts – "for we mourn not as those without hope, for them that sleep in Him" – seemed to him to have a new and deeper meaning. For he felt that not only was his little Nelly safe, but that he, too, was secure in the almighty love of God.

For several weeks Joe hardly knew at times whether he was in the body or out of it. Wrapped in contemplation, he would forget "all time and toil and care," and the long nights would slip away like a dream. He grew more silent than ever; but the look of melancholy was rapidly disappearing from his weatherbeaten face, and an expression of heart-rest and peace was taking its place.

But one morning, as Joe was walking home from his work, lost as usual in contemplation, a thought crossed his mind that fairly startled him, and for several moments he stood stock-still in the street.

"Oh, dear! oh, dear!" he groaned. "If I don't desarve to be reprobated, my name's not Joe Wrag."

Then he walked on again with rapid strides, as if he would escape the haunting thought. But the thought would not leave him; nay, it seemed to grow into a living voice, that sounded clear and distinct above the roar of the streets.

"Joe Wrag," it said, "is your religion such a selfish thing, and is your joy such a selfish thing, that you can think of nothing but yourself? Are you the only one for whom Christ died? Are there no tired and toil-worn men and women around you struggling in the darkness and longing for light? Do you want heaven all to yourself, that you invite no one to go along with you? For shame, Joe Wrag, you are actually growing selfish! In your thankfulness that you have found a place of shelter, you have forgotten the many outside still exposed to the storm. Is this what you have learnt of Christ? Get down on your knees, man, and ask His pardon, and ask Him for grace also that you may be saved from yourself, and that henceforth you may live for Christ and humanity."

"O Lord, have marcy!" cried Joe, rushing on faster and faster. "I've been as blind as a bat, an as selfish as sin could make me. Enter not into judgment with me for Thy marcy's sake, an' I'll try to do better – I will, for sure."

When Joe reached his home, he went at once to his bedroom, and falling on his knees, he poured out his soul in a long and agonising prayer. He prayed for grace and strength, he prayed for light and wisdom. He did not ask for peace or joy, but he asked to be made holy and useful, that he might do diligently his life-work, and be able to say when death came, "I have finished the work that Thou gavest me to do."

When Joe came downstairs a light was shining in his eyes, such as his wife (who had been for many years Joe's "thorn in the flesh") had never seen before.

From that day Joe Wrag was a changed man, and, as might be expected, his wife was the first to notice the change and the first to appreciate it. That very morning, instead of eating his meal in silence, as had been his custom for many years, he began to talk to her, to ask her questions, and to interest himself in domestic affairs. And when he had taken his four or five hours' sleep, instead of moping in silence, as he had been in the habit of doing, until it was time to go to his work, he actually began to help his wife to tidy up the house, and even anticipated her wants in several little matters, and altogether made himself so agreeable that his wife was at her wits' end to know what had come over him.

Mary Wrag had grown, as the years had slipped by, from a light-hearted, high-spirited girl, into a sour, disappointed, and vixenish woman. Poor Joe was utterly at a loss to understand the change that had come over her. He could not think that he had contributed to it in the smallest degree. He had never crossed her, never answered her back when she snarled at him, never bothered her with his own troubles, and never vexed her by trying to pry into hers. He had always let her have her own way, and had scarcely interfered with her in anything, and hence it was a mystery to him how she had grown so cross-grained and sour.

It was a very common mistake, and one that has been fraught with the most serious results. He did not know how, in the years gone by, his wife had longed to share his troubles (for she was too proud to tell him), and how she wanted him to share hers. He did not know what a trouble it was to her when he sat hour after hour moody and silent, never speaking to her, and taking no interest in anything she did or said. He did not know what bitter tears she shed in the early years of their wedded life, because he would not notice a new bow of pink ribbon she had made, or a new fashion in which she had done up her glossy hair.

"I don't believe," she would say bitterly, "that Joe cares a bit what I wears. It's not a bit of pleasure to try an' make oneself look nice, for he never notices."

And so she grew cross and sour. He never blamed her, it is true, but she complained to herself that he never praised her, and even when she got thoroughly out of temper, and gave him, a good "blowing up," his silence only exasperated her all the more.

"I'd rather a thousan' times over," she would say, "that he'd get cross, an' answer back again, than sit still, turnin' up his eyes like a dyin' dolphin."

Had Joe known all this, it would certainly have been a great trouble to him, and yet if he had known it, it would doubtless have saved him many years of pain.

But after the morning to which we have alluded, Joe's conduct and manner changed in a remarkable degree. He became thoughtful and attentive and communicative, and he began to think, too, that his wife's temper was improving; and after a few weeks he was surprised at the wonderful change that had come over her, little dreaming that it was the change in himself that had produced the change in his wife.

The experiment to which we alluded in the opening sentences of this chapter was that of trying to get hold of his neighbours and acquaintances, and helping them if possible to a higher and better life. There were people living all round him – some of them he had known for twenty years – who never went to church or chapel, and who seemed utterly unconcerned about death and the great hereafter that lay beyond it – people whose life was one hopeless round of toil, with nothing to brighten or cheer its dull monotony. Some of them were decent people too, honest and industrious. It is true they got drunk occasionally, and were not always as civil to their wives and families and to each other as they might be; yet, notwithstanding, they had a soft place in their hearts, and were ever ready to watch by a sick neighbour's bed-side, or lend a helping hand to a mate more needy than themselves.

How to get hold of these children of the great Father, and lead them into His fold, was a problem that had puzzled Joe for some time. At length he decided, with his wife's consent, to invite them to tea, or as many of them as could be accommodated, some Sunday afternoon, and when he had got them together, to talk to them on those matters which were of such vital importance.

Accordingly the invitations were sent out, and on the Sunday afternoon already mentioned some fifteen men found their way to Joe Wrag's cottage, wondering what was in the wind.

When they had all got comfortably seated on the forms that Joe had provided, Joe stood up in a corner of the room, and looked around him: evidently it was no easy task to begin to talk. Joe had no idea that it would be so difficult. Every eye was fixed upon him with a wondering expression. Joe coughed two or three times, then making a tremendous effort, he said, "You all know me, mates?"

"Ay," they all exclaimed, "we ought to, anyhow."

"Ay, jist so," said Joe, feeling more at ease now that the ice was broken; "but I've discovered lately, lads, that I ain't a-done my duty."

"Come, old boss, we ain't a-blamin' yer; so don't begin a ballyraggin' yoursel' in that way," said one of the men.

"Facts is stubborn, though," went on Joe, "an' I see that I've kep' mysel' too much to mysel', an' I ain't a-been that neighbourly as I ought to ha' been; but I intend to do differ'nt."

"Well, I'm hanged," said the man who had before spoken, "if I ain't considerable at a loss, Joe, to know what yer drivin' at."

"I'spects so, no doubt, but I'm not good at 'splainin'; but it 'pears to me, mates, as how we ain't got hold o' life by the right end."

"Yer mean *us*, Joe?" questioned several voices together.

"Well, p'r'aps I do. You don't git much comfort in this life, and yer ain't preparin' for a better life. Don't stop me; but I used to think that heaven wern't for me, and for lots o' us poor chaps – that we didn't belong to the elect; but, bless

134

yer, lads, I know now that the elect are everybody as likes. We are all God's children, an' He loves us all, the bad 'uns as well as the good 'uns, an' He's promised pardon an' heaven to whosoever will. Let me tell 'e, lads, how it came about. A little girl an' her brother comed an' axed me to let 'em warm theirselves by my fire one pinchin' cold night. A purtier little critter than little Nelly never breathed, wi' her great round eyes an' sweet mouth. I seem to see her now, though she's asleep in her grave. Well, when her father druv 'em from home, I got a place for 'em wi' Betty Barker. An' Betty used to read to 'em out o' the Testament. An' then they got into a chapel, an' heerd a couple o' sermons – leastaway Nelly did; the lad were asleep durin' the preachin'. Well, you can't tell how eager that little gal became to know more about the Saviour, an' heaven, an' all the rest o' it. An' she used to come an' ax me all sorts o' questions. Bless yer, that little girl had real speretuel insight; she used to floor me complete. I never heerd sich posers as she used to put sometimes. But I tell 'e, mates, every one of the questions helped to lead me out o' the darkness into the light. Day after day it got clearer, an' yet I doubted. I spoke the promises to the little gal, and yet I were afeard to take 'em mysel'. I had a vision, too, one night, an' that helped me amazin'. But not until my little Nell was dyin' did I see clear. The nurse said to me what she seed the little gal wanted to say, an' that took down the last shutter, an' the light streamed in. I can't tell yer all the joys, lads, I've felt, but for a long time I kept it all to mysel'. But the Lord has showed to me how selfish I've been, an' now I want for everybody to get close to the Saviour."

For a moment there was silence, then one of the men said, "But there's wussur chaps 'n us goin'."

"Ay, that's true, lad," said Joe; "but you're all bad

enough to be better, an' the Saviour wants 'e all to be – good, an' He wants to help 'e all to be patient an' bear the burden of life, an' He wants to show 'e how much He loves an' cares for 'e all."

"I dunna think He ken love us very much," said one of the men sullenly, "or He wouldn't ha' put us in this 'ere muck all our lives."

"Well, lads," replied Joe thoughtfully, "I 'fess I can't 'splain all. An' the Book tells us how we on'y see through a glass darkly. We looks at life an' the world an' everything through a smoked glass, an' it all 'pears dark. But I tell 'e, lads, this I know, that God loves us, ay, loves us, and He'll make everything right and square by-and-bye, if we will only leave it wi' Him."

"I dunna see much sign o' the love anywheres," said the man in reply.

"P'r'aps so," said Joe. "But yer see, mates, as how sin an' the devil have comed in th' world, an' they's made terrible mischief, terrible, and many o' us 'as bin 'elping the devil all we could, an' so between us we's got oursels into a queer scrape, an' piled misery an' sorrow o' top o' our 'eads. But God loved us so much that He sent the Saviour to take away our sin an' make us free. An' yet all the time we complain as if our Father made all the mischief an' trouble, when most o' us 'as a-made it oursels."

"Ay, that's true, lad," said Dick Somerset, the man that had spoken most.

"Course it are true," said Joe, brightening up. "An', besides, it may be a good thing for us to be kep' poor an' 'ave plenty o' 'ard work. The Lord knows best, you may depend on't, what's best for us; lots of us couldn't stand riches, 't would be the greatest curse we could 'ave. I b'lieve if you place some people on a hoss they'd ride to the devil, but if you were to keep 'em in clogs they'd plod on all the way to Paradise."

"It's 'nation 'ard, though," said several of the men, "to be allers a-grindin' away at it as we's bound to do."

"Ay, lads," said Joe, "that are true, an' yet I reckon we ain't a-tried very much to better our position. Some o' yer 'as spent in drink what yer might a-saved, an' if yer 'ad a-done so, an' 'ad spent yer evenin's improvin' yer mind an' gettin' some larnin', ye might ha' been better off. I might, I see it now quite clear; but as I said at the fust, we's 'ad hold o' life by the wrong end. An' I wants us all to begin afresh."

"But how is we to do it, Joe?" said several voices.

"Well, let's begin by axin' the Lord for pardon for all the past, an' for strength to do better for the future."

And Joe got down upon his knees at once and began to pray, and while he pleaded the promises, it seemed to him as if the little room became full of the presence of the Most High. All his hesitancy of speech vanished. It seemed to him as if he had got hold of the very hand of God, and he cried out, "I will not let Thee go until Thou bless me." Promise after promise crowded into his mind with more rapidity than he could utter them; until at length, overcome by his feelings, he cried out, "I canna doubt, I canna doubt no more!" then he hid his face in his hands, and there was silence throughout the room. When he rose from his knees his face fairly shone with joy, and the men looked wonderingly at him and at each other.

Just then there was a knock at the little kitchen door, and Joe's wife came in to say that she was waiting to bring in the tea.

"Right thee are, lass," said Joe. "I'd nearly forgotten the tea; bring it away as fast as thee likes."

And Mary Wrag and a neighbour's wife who had come in

to help began to bring in large plates of cake and bread and butter, which the men greedily devoured. It was very evident that whatever they thought of the other part of the service, they enjoyed this part of it.

Joe was more pleased than he could tell at his experiment, and from that day every Sunday afternoon his house was thrown open to any of his neighbours who might like to come in, and hear the Bible read, and have a little conversation about spiritual things.

It was wonderful, now that the tongue of this silent man had been unloosed, how freely he could talk, and he never lacked a congregation. The neighbours flocked to hear him talk of Jesus and of His wondrous love, and in Joe's little kitchen many a weary and heavy-laden soul found peace and rest.

In a little Bethel near his home Joe found a place to worship God. He loved now to be in the house of prayer. It no longer gave him pain to talk of heaven and of the joys of the redeemed, for he knew that heaven was open to him, and that in a little while he would find again the little angel that led him into the light, and look upon the Saviour whom he loved.

CHAPTER XVII

Perks Again

I knew, I knew it could not last;
'T was bright, 't was heavenly, but 't is past.
Oh, ever thus from childhood's hour
I've seen my fondest hopes decay.
I never nursed a tree or flower,
But 't was the first to fade away;
I never nursed a dear gazelle
To glad me with its soft black eye,
But when it came to know me well,
And love me, it was sure to die.

Moore

ON the Monday morning Benny was brought before the magistrates charged with stealing five pounds from his master's office. He was almost ready to faint when placed in the dock; but, conscious of his own innocence, he gathered up his courage, and answered fearlessly the questions that were addressed to him.

Inspector Sharp gave the particulars of the case, adding that though the money had not been found on the prisoner, or indeed anywhere else, yet he had no doubt that the lad had accomplices to whom he had given the missing property.

Benny denied most emphatically that he had seen the

money: he admitted that appearances were against him. "But, oh," he said, looking at the presiding magistrate, his eyes swimming with tears, "I'm not a thief, sir, if you'll on'y believe it; I'm not, really."

Benny's honest face and simple straightforward answers evidently made in his favour; but as Mr. Lawrence had not appeared against him, he was remanded until the following day, so he was removed once more to his cell.

Perks' case was not tried that day, so once more Benny had him for a companion.

During most of the evening Perks sat in one corner, with his face in his hands, and his elbows on his knees, without either speaking or moving. Benny took the opposite corner, glad for once that he had a chance of being quiet. He wondered what would be done to him, whether he would be sent to prison or set at liberty. He felt that he did not care much what happened, for to be penned up in prison, he thought, could not be much worse than to go back in disgrace to the old life of selling matches in the streets.

Above the grated window the little patch of blue began to fade as the day waned and darkened into night. Then a solitary star appeared, and looked down with kindly eye into the dreary cell. Benny watched the star twinkling so far above him, and wondered what it could be. Was it one of God's eyes, or the eye of one of His angels? Could it be his Nelly that was looking at him? Or were the stars only holes in the floor of heaven to let the glory through?

He could not tell, but somehow that kindly star looking in upon him seemed to comfort his heart; and he felt that though the world buffeted him, and would not give him a chance of getting on, yet he was not forgotten of God.

Then his thoughts turned to Perks. Was God watching him also? for the star was not visible from the corner where he crouched. Why was he so quiet? Was he sorry for what he had done, or was he ill?

Benny was glad to be quiet; and yet somehow as the darkness deepened he felt lonesome, and wondered what had come to the silent figure in the corner. It was so unusual for Perks to be quiet so long. He listened for a moment, but all was still. And still the minutes dragged away, and the silence became oppressive.

"Perks!" said Benny, unable longer to keep quiet; and his voice awoke the sleeping echoes of the cell, and made it sound hollow as a tomb.

But the echoes were his only answer.

"Perks!" in a louder voice.

Still there was silence, and Benny began to get frightened. Was he dead? he wondered. How awful it would be to be in that cell all night alone with a dead body!

"Perks, do speak!" in a tone of agony.

And he listened for an answer, while the perspiration stood in great drops upon his forehead. But still only silence. He could hear the thumping of his own heart distinctly, and he became hot and cold by turns with fright.

At length he thought he heard a noise coming from the corner where he felt sure Perks was crouched dead. It sounded like suppressed laughter. What could it mean? He dared not move from his corner. Was it Satan come to carry away Perks? for he was very wicked, he knew.

It had got too dark now to see anything distinctly; but there was a shuffling noise on the floor. Horrors! it was coming across the cell towards him. What was it? He could see some unshapely thing moving. Now it was drawing itself up to its full height. Benny nearly shrieked out in an agony of terror. Then it flashed across his mind in a moment – Perks was playing him another of his tricks.

Waiting until Perks was near enough, he dealt him a blow straight from the shoulder that sent him sprawling to the other end of the cell.

"Oh, for a massy!" he shouted, "if that ain't a stinger!"

"Serves you right." said Benny.

"Lor, but didn't I give you a scarin', just! I never did injoy a thing as much in my life; but, oh, lor! I nearly busted once or twice wi' larfin'."

"I think I gived you a scarin' too," retorted Benny.

"Well, I confess it comed raather sudden like; so that's one to you, Ben. I'll give you yer due."

"I've a good mind to pound you to a jelly," said Benny. "Yer always on with yer tricks."

"Well, I didn't 'tend to scare yer, Ben, for I wur bissy medertatin' on a little plan I 'as in my yed; but when yer spoke 'Perks!' anxious like, the idear comed to me all in a moment. Oh, lor, weren't it a spree!"

"I don't see no fun in it," said Benny.

"Oh, lor, yer don't?" and Perks laughed again. "But I say, Ben, I wants yer 'elp in carryin' out as purty a bit o' play as ever you seen."

"Is it what you've been thinking about all the evenin'?"

"Ay, lad, it's the most butifullest idear that wur ever 'atched in this 'ere noddle; an' if you'll only 'elp me, my stars! our fortin's made."

"You're up to no good again, I'll be bound," said Benny.

"Well, I reckon you'll alter yer mind on that score when yer 'ears the details o' my plan," said Perks, coming closer to Benny's side.

"Well, what is it?"

"I must whisper it," said Perks, "though I dunna thinks any bobbies is around listenin' at this time o' night, but it's allers best to be on the safe side."

"I don't want to 'ear it," said Benny, "if it's some'at you must whisper. It's no good, that I'm sartin of."

"Don't be a ninny, Ben. Just listen."

And Perks confided to Ben a plan of getting into the house of an old man who kept a little shop, and lived all alone, and who kept all his money locked up in a little cupboard in the room behind the shop.

"How do you know he keeps his money there?" said Benny.

"Never you mind," was the answer; "I does know it to a sartinty."

"Where does the old man live?"

"No. 86 ------- Street."

"What's his name?"

"Jerry Starcher. Ain't yer 'eard o' 'im?"

"Ay," said Benny.

"Then you'll 'elp?" said Perks, eagerly.

"Ay," said Benny, "but not in the way you thinks."

"What does yer mean?"

"I mean, if I get out of this place, I'll put the old man on his guard."

"What, an' split on me?"

"No, I'll not mention names."

"Then I 'opes ye'll be sent to a 'formatory an' kep' there for the next five year."

"Do you? Why?"

"'Cause yer a fool, Ben Bates."

"How so?"

"'Cause ye are, I say."

"Well, your saying so don't make it so, anyhow," retorted Benny.

"Don't it, though? But look 'ere: ye're 'ere for stealin', and I can tell yer from 'sperience, that a gent as takes up the

143

perfession is worse nor a fool to give it up agin 'cause he
'appens to get nabbed."

"But I'm not here for stealin'," said Benny, colouring.

"Ye're not, eh?" said Perks, laughing till the tears ran
down his face. "Well, that are the richest bit I's heard for the
last month."

"But," said Benny, with flashing eyes, "though I'm here
charged with stealing, I tell yer I'm honest."

"Are that a fact, now, Ben?" said Perks, looking serious.

"It is," replied Benny; "I never took the money."

"Well, so much the worse," said Perks.

"How's that?"

"'Cause yer might as well be a thief, hout an' hout, as be
charged wi' bein' one. I tell 'e there's no chance for yer: the
bobbies'll 'ave their eyes on yer wherever yer be; and if yer
gits a sitivation they'll come along an' say to yer guv'nor,
'Yon's a jail-bird, yer'd better 'ave yer eye on 'im;' then yell
'ave to walk it somewheres else, an' it'll be the same
everywheres."

"How do you know that?" said Benny.

"'Cause I's 'sperienced it," was the reply. "I's older 'n
you, though you's biggest; but I reckons as I knows most,
an' it's true what I say. Why, bless yer, the first time I ever
nabbed I got a month, an' I wor so horful frightened, that I
vowed if ever I got out I'd be honest, an' never get in no
more; but, bless yer, it wur no go. The bobbies told each
ether who I wur, an' they was always a-watching me. I got a
sitivation once, a honcommon good 'un, too; but, oh, lor, the
next day a bobby says to the guv'nor, says he, 'Yon's a jail-
bird, you'd better keep yer eye on 'm;' an' you may guess
I'd to walk in quick sticks. I made two or three tries arter,
but it wur no go. As soon as hever a bobby came near I'd to
be off like greased lightnin', and you'll find out what I say.

If yer not a thief now, ye'll 'ave to come to it. I tell yer there's no help for it."

"But I tell you I'll *not* come to it," said Benny, stoutly.

"But I knows better," persisted Perks; "there ken be no possible chance for yer. Ye're down, an' the world'll keep 'e down, though yer try ever so."

Benny looked thoughtful, for he had a suspicion that a good deal that Perks said was true. He was down, and he feared there was very little, if any, chance of his getting up again. He had proved by experience that the world was hard upon poor lads, and he knew it would be doubly hard upon him now that his character was gone. Yet he felt that he could not become a thief. He would sooner die, and he told Perks so.

But Perks only laughed at the idea.

"You'll find that dyin' ain't so precious easy, my lad," he said, in a patronising tone of voice. And Benny felt that very likely Perks' words were true in relation to that matter, and so he was silent.

"You'd better come partner 'long wi' me," said Perks, in a tone of voice that was intended to be encouraging.

"No," said Benny. "I'll help you if you'll try to be honest; for look here, Perks: there's another life besides this, an' if we're not good we shall go to the bad place when we die, for only good people can go to heaven. An' I want to go to the good place, for little Nell is there; an' I want to see her again, for she was all I had to love in the world, an' oh! it 'ud grieve her so if I were to be a thief, an' grieve the good Lord who died for us all. No, Perks, little Nell begged me afore she died to be good, an' she said the Lord 'ud provide, an' I means to be good. Won't you try to be good, too, Perks? I'm sure it 'ud be better."

"No," said Perks: "folks 'as druv' me to what I is. I tried

145

to be honest once, an' they wouldn't let me, an' so I intends to stick to the perfession now, for I likes it; an' ye'll come to it yet."

"I'd rather die," said Benny solemnly.

"Humbug!" snarled Perks. "But I'll say this afore I go to sleep, for I's gettin' despert sleepy, if ye'll join me in the perfession I'll be a frien' to yer, an' put yer up to all the tricks, an' forgive yer for that hidin' yer give me. But if," and he brought out the words slowly, "ye'll 'sist on bein' a fool, I'll pay off old scores yet, and I'll plague yer worst norever I's done yet! so I give yer fair warnin'. Now for the land o' nod."

Neither of them spoke again after that, and soon after they were both locked in the arms of kindly sleep.

The following morning Benny was again brought before the magistrates, but nothing new was brought forward in evidence. Mr. Lawrence, however, stated that he did not wish to prosecute, or in any way punish the lad. And as there was no positive evidence that Benny had taken the money, he was dismissed. It was evident, however, that the general belief was that he was guilty; but as the evidence was only presumptive, and this being his first appearance before them, he was given the benefit of the doubt, and set at liberty, with a caution that if he came before them again he would not get off so easily.

His week's wages that Mr. Lawrence had paid him was restored to him on leaving the court, and once more he found himself a homeless orphan on the streets of Liverpool.

Perks did not fare so well. He was an old and evidently a hardened offender. The case was also proved against him, and he was sentenced to be kept in prison for three calendar months. Perks heard the sentence unmoved. He liked liberty best, it is true, but the only thing that grieved him was that it was summertime. If it had been winter, he would not have cared a straw; but as it was he was determined to make the best of it, and get as much enjoyment out of it as he possibly could.

So Perks and Benny drifted apart, and Benny wondered if they would ever meet again. Life before him lay dark and cheerless. He seemed to have drifted away from everything: no friend was left to him in all the world. There were granny and Joe, but he could not see them, for he felt that if a shade of suspicion crept into their manner, it would break his heart. No, he would keep away. Then there was Mr. Lawrence; he could expect nothing further from him. He believed him to be a thief, of that there could be no doubt, and so doubtless did Morgan and all the other clerks. And then there was little Eva, the angel that had brightened his life for six brief months, and whose bright shilling nothing could induce him to part with. Did she believe him guilty too? Of course she did. His guilt must seem so clear to every one of them. And so he was alone in the world, without a friend to help, unless God would help him; but of that he did not feel quite sure. Sometimes he thought that the Lord would surely provide, but at other times he doubted.

He was at liberty, it was true, and ought he not to be thankful for that? he asked himself; but alas! his innocence had not been established. Young as he was, he felt the force of that. And he felt it terribly hard that all – all! even his little angel – believed him to be a thief.

Ah! he did not know how sore was Eva Lawrence's little heart, and how she persisted to her father that Benny was innocent, and pleaded with him, but pleaded in vain, for him to take back the poor boy and give him another chance.

And night after night she cried herself to sleep as she

thought of the little orphan sent adrift on life's treacherous ocean, and wondered what the end would be. And when one day she tried to sing "Love at Home," the words almost choked her, for the pleading, suffering face of the homeless child came up before her, and looked at her with hungry wistful eyes, as if asking for sympathy and help.

But children soon forget their griefs, and as the days wore away, and lengthened into weeks, Benny was almost forgotten, till one day a circumstance occurred which made him again the talk of the Lawrence household. What that circumstance was shall be told in its proper place in the unfolding of this story of Benny's life.

CHAPTER XVIII

Adrift

A fathomless sea is rolling
O'er the wreck of the bravest bark
And my pain-muffled heart is tolling
Its dumb peal down in the dark.

The waves of a mighty sorrow
Have 'whelmed the pearl of my life;
And there cometh to me no morrow,
To solace this desolate strife.

Gone are the last faint flashes,
Set is the sun of my years;
And over a few poor ashes
I sit in my darkness and tears.

Gerald Massey

HAD any of our readers been passing the front of St.
George's Hall during the afternoon of the day on which
Benny was acquitted, they might have seen our hero sitting
on one of the many steps, with his face buried in his hands
and his elbows resting on his knees. Hour after hour he sat
unmolested, for Perks was no longer at liberty to tease him,
and the police did not notice him.

Benny was utterly unconscious of the flight of time, for
he was trying to decide upon some course of action by

which he could honestly earn his daily bread. He felt that he was beginning life again, and beginning it under tremendous disadvantages. He knew that there was a great deal of truth in what Perks had said to him. All who knew him would mistrust him, and even should he succeed in getting employment under those who did not know him, they might soon get to know, and then he would be dismissed. He was getting too big to be a match boy. He did not understand blacking shoes, and yet to remain idle meant starvation.

"I'm wuss nor a chap buried," he said to himself, thrusting his hands into his trousers pockets and staring around him. "I've heerd of chaps beginnin' at the bottom, but lor a massy! I'm beginnin' furder down than that by a long chalk. I'm six feet under ground, an' I'll 'ave to bore a hole up inter the daylight, or die, I'specks."

As the afternoon wore away he became conscious of a feeling of hunger. Fortunately, he had sufficient money to keep him from starving for a day or two. He counted over the coins very carefully, and laid aside eighteen pence as being due to granny, and which he resolved should be paid.

"I'll begin honest," he said to himself, "an' I'll keep on at it too, or go to heaven to little Nell."

So after purchasing two sheets of paper and two envelopes, he made his way to a small eating-house and ordered some bread and cheese. He was not long in devouring his very simple meal, and then with a lead pencil commenced his first attempt at letter-writing. The first letter contained only a few words of warning to Jerry Starcher. The second letter was longer, and was addressed to granny. This letter cost Benny a tremendous effort, for, fearing that granny would not be able to read writing, he had, to use his own words, "to print it," and he found it to be a rather slow process. The letter was to the following effect:

"DEER GRANY, – I ken never come 'ome no more. You's heerd what's took plaas, but I newer stole the money. I is 'onest, for shure I dunno wat I'll do or whair I'll go; but I meen to be 'onest or die. I wish I wur ded. I is very, very, very 'bliged for ale you's, don for me an' littel Nel: tel Joe I is 'bliged to 'im to. P'r'aps I'll never see 'e no more, p'r'aps I'll go to littel Nel soon. I 'ope I may, I's very lon-ly. I put with this the money I ow's. Good nite. – BENNY."

More than one scalding tear fell upon the letter while he wrote, for the tears would come despite his efforts to keep them back. Life seemed to him such an utter desolation, and hope had almost died out of his heart.

When he had carefully folded and sealed the letters, he went out again on the steps in the shadow of the great Hall, and waited for the darkness. All around him the people hurried to and fro. But had he been in the heart of Africa he could not have felt more utterly forsaken and alone.

When at length the darkness crept over the busy town, he hurried away to Tempest Court, passing Jerry Starcher's, and pushing the letter under his door on the way. His heart beat very fast when he reached granny's door. He was strongly tempted to knock for admittance, for something told him that granny would not turn him away, but he struggled against the feeling. Welcome as would have been his little bed under the stairs, and glad as he would have been for a hiding-place from the world's scorn, yet he felt he would rather not see granny and Joe again while this stain darkened his name.

Within the cottage silence and darkness reigned, for granny had retired early to rest – not without a prayer, though, that the boy she was learning to love might see the error of his ways, truly repent of his sin, and lead a new life. For Joe had told her what had befallen Benny, and furthermore had extracted from her the promise that if he should ever seek again the shelter of her home, for his little sister's sake and for the sake of the Saviour, she would not turn him away, but would help him to begin a better life.

Benny listened for a while at the key-hole, then cautiously pushing the letter under the door, he hurried away into the darkness. He had no idea where he would spend the night, nor did he concern himself about the direction he was taking; he only felt that he must go somewhere. So on he went in a northerly direction, passing street after street, till, footsore and weary, he stumbled into a dark corner where he thought nobody would notice him, and soon fell fast asleep.

Why could not the policeman who passed half an hour later, and spied the little crouching figure, have permitted the child to sleep on? He was doing no harm, and the policeman might have known that had the boy a home to go to he would not have been found sleeping in the street.

I suppose he thought nothing about the matter, for he seized Benny by the collar and lifted him off the ground, and after shaking him as a terrier might shake a rat, he ordered him to move on, giving emphasis to his words by a cruel kick, which made Benny grind his teeth with pain, and hurry limping down the street.

He had not gone far before a clock near him began to strike slowly the hour of midnight. At the first stroke of the bell Benny started, and looked carefully around him. Clang went the second stroke.

"It must be the same," he muttered to himself.

The third stroke made him certain.

He was near Addler's Hall without knowing it. The tone of the church clock was as familiar to him as the voice of his father. Scores of times during the years of his childhood he had listened to that clang, waking up the midnight silence when all the others were asleep.

"I wonder if father's comed home yet?" he said to himself; "I'll go and see, anyhow."

Bowker's Row was as silent as the grave, and, as usual, wrapped in darkness. But the darkness was no difficulty to Benny, as he made his way cautiously up the dingy street and into the dingier court that was once his home. It seemed very strange to him that he should be there alone in the silent night, and that Nelly should be alone in her little grave miles away from where he stood.

What a lot had been crowded into his lonely life since last he stood in Addler's Hall, holding his little sister by the hand! And he wondered if ever Nelly left her beautiful home in the sky to pay a visit to the dreary haunts of her childhood.

Before him the door of his old home stood open – the night was not so dark but he could see that – and he could see also that the place wore even a more forsaken appearance than in former days.

Pausing for a moment on the threshold, he plunged into the darkness, then stood still in the middle of the room and listened; but no sound of breathing or noise of any kind broke the oppressive stillness.

He soon discovered also that the house was destitute of furniture; a few shavings under the stairs alone remained.

"The bobbies'll not find me 'ere, I reckon," he said to himself, "though Nelly may."

And he stretched himself on the shavings in the corner where he and his little sister used to sleep in the days that had gone for ever.

It seemed so strange to be there again, and to be there in sorrow and disgrace; and once or twice he stretched out his hand in the darkness as if expecting to find his little sister by his side. Then, as the memory of his loss and the loneliness of his life crept over him, he gave vent to his feelings in a flood of tears. By-and-bye he grew calm, and soon after fell asleep; and in happy dreams, in which he wandered with Nelly through Eastham Woods, he forgot all his trouble and care.

When he awoke the next morning the court was alive and stirring, and Bowker's Row was crowded with ill-fed, ragged, and dirty children: some were doing their best to climb the lamp-posts, some were practising cart-wheel revolutions, some were squatted idly on the pavement, and others were playing with the refuse in the street.

On Benny making his appearance, he was greeted with a shout and a howl that made the street echo again, and summoned the elders to the doorways to see what had happened.

It was very evident that the older children had recognised him, while many a familiar face appeared at door and window. This Benny thought was very unfortunate, for he was in no mood to be questioned or to brook delay. So he darted down the street as if on a race for life, knocking over several of the older lads who tried to check his progress.

For some distance he was followed by a whole tribe of noisy urchins, who shouted at the top of their voices. But Benny was too fleet-footed for them, and soon Bowker's Row and its noisy denizens were left far behind.

Benny's first thought now was to secure a substantial

breakfast, which was by no means a difficult matter. That done, he made his way toward the docks, in the hope that he might get employment of some kind. But to a little friendless lad, without character or recommendation, employment was not so easily obtained. Most of those whom he addressed did not condescend to notice his question in any way. A few asked him what he could do, and when he replied "Anything," the invariable answer was, "That means nothing," and he was sent about his business. In fact, there seemed to be no work in the whole line of docks that a child of his age was capable of doing. And night found him worn out with fatigue, and with a sadly lightened pocket.

However, he kept up his heart as well as he could, and sought rest and sleep in a damp cellar upon some dirty straw, which for the payment of twopence he shared with a dozen other lads, who appeared to be as friendless as himself. That night he slept the sleep of the innocent and weary, and awoke next morning, strengthened and refreshed, to find that all his companions had left and that his pockets were empty!

This was a terrible blow to Benny; but when he discovered that his "lucky shilling" was still safe in the lining of his waistcoat, he dried his tears, and went bravely out, hungry as he was, to battle with an unfriendly world.

Before sunset, however, he had nearly lost heart, for he had been unable to earn a single penny, and he was almost faint with hunger. So in sheer desperation he sought his old place on the landing-stage, in the hope that he might have the chance of carrying someone's portmanteau, and in that way earn his supper; but every one to whom he offered his service repulsed him, and for the first time he wondered whether it would be wrong to throw himself into the river, and whether that would not be the easiest way out of his trouble. Somehow he could not help thinking that it would be less wicked for him to do that than to steal. He could not starve; drowning he was sure would be a much less painful death; and, as far as he could see, it had really come to this, that he must either steal or die. But he would not steal, he had made up his mind to that. Had he not promised Nelly that he would be honest? And had not Joe and granny and his Sunday-school teacher told him what a wicked thing it was to be a thief? No; he had settled that matter, and when he had settled a thing in his own mind he was not to be moved. The question then was, what was the easiest kind of death? The river looked beautiful this summer evening, and he thought it must be very nice to rest beneath its cool sparkling waters after the hot glare of the streets. Should he plunge in now, or should he wait a little longer? He had been without food for twenty-four hours. He had no place to sleep, no means of getting supper.

Then suddenly he remembered his "lucky shilling".

"Queer!" he mused. "The Lord sent His angel wi' this bob, an' I've never wanted it till now, an' now I does want it, I've got it. I'm floored again. Nelly said the Lord 'ud provide, and He do." And he took out the bright shilling and looked at it fondly.

Just then he heard a countryman inquiring the way to Lime Street Station, of a man who stood near him.

"Here's a chance," he thought; and, stepping forward, he said, "I'll show you the way, sir, if yer likes."

"Dost thee know th' way thysel', lad?" inquired the man.

"I should think I do," said Benny, drawing himself up to his full height.

"Lead the way, then," said the farmer; and Benny trotted on before him, feeling sure that he was safe now for a good supper without spending his shilling.

"Thankee," said the farmer, on their arrival at the station; "thee'rt a sharp lad, an' no mistake."

And he smiled benevolently, and hurried away to the booking-office, leaving our hero staring after him in utter bewilderment.

Benny felt that he would have liked to have had his revenge on that man then and there.

"Golly," he said, "don't I feel savage, just!"

Just then a gentleman pushed against him, carrying a bulky leathern bag.

"Carry yer bag, sir?" said Benny in an instant; and, without a word, the bag was hoisted on his shoulder, and once more Benny was on the trot.

By the time he had reached the top of Brownlow Hill he was almost exhausted, and without a word the man (gentleman, I suppose he thought himself) took the bag from his shoulder and handed him a penny in payment for his services.

When, will men, and professedly Christian men, learn the great though simple lesson to do unto others as they would that others should do unto them?

A benevolent baker, moved to pity by the sight of Benny's suffering face, gave him a twopenny loaf for his penny, with a smile and a kindly word into the bargain, and Benny went out into the darkening street with a lighter heart than he had felt for the day.

The evening was oppressively warm, and having no inclination to go back again into the dingy town, where policemen were plentiful, Benny made his way in an easterly direction, hoping that he might find a dark corner somewhere where he might sleep undisturbed.

After a while he found himself in the neighbourhood of

the cemetery where Nelly was buried. He was not superstitious, so without a moment's hesitation he climbed over the wall, and, getting dark as it was, he easily found his sister's grave; and, stretching himself on the damp grass, with his head upon the little mound under which his Nelly slept in peace, he tried to think – to form some plan for the future.

Above him twinkled the silent stars. Around him slept the silent dead. Everything was silent; not a leaf stirred, not even a blade of grass; and yielding to the silent influence of the hour, he fell asleep, though not before he had resolved that he would return to his old haunts no more, but would commence his new life as far away from Liverpool as he could possibly get.

Next morning he was up with the lark, and kissing the sod above his sister's face, he hurried away. At noon Liverpool was several miles behind him, and before him – what?

Under the shadow of a tree by the roadside he rested for an hour during the heat of the day; and in a clear stream that babbled by he slaked his thirst and washed the dust from his hands and face, then hurried on again.

The country looked very beautiful bathed in the summer's sunshine, but he was in no mood to enjoy it. The birds sang their glad songs in the trees, but to him they seemed only to mock his sorrow. In fields he saw the sleek cattle grazing as he passed, or lying in the sunshine contentedly chewing cud, while he was footsore, hungry, and sad, and he wondered what the end of it all would be.

As the afternoon wore away he found himself hedged in with plantations on every side, and not a single human habitation in sight.

For a while he dragged himself along with fast failing courage and strength; then he gave up in despair.

"It's no go," he said; "I ken go no furder."

His feet were hot and blistered with his long tramp over the hard and dusty road. His head ached from the fierce heat that had been beating down on him all the day, his strength was all but gone, for he had tasted no food since the previous evening.

"I dunno how the Lord's goin' to do it," he said, the tears starting in his eyes. "Nelly said as how the Lord 'ud provide, an' so did the angel that gived me the bob; but I dunna see how. I wonder if He's goin' to take me to heaven? P'r'aps that's the way He's goin' to do it, an' then I'll never be 'ungry no more."

Climbing on a gate, he looked around him, but no house was anywhere visible.

"It's all up, I reckon," he said sadly, getting down on the inside and making his way through the tangled undergrowth into the heart of the plantation.

I'll find a snug place 'ere somewheres, where I ken wait till the Lord comes. I wonder if He'll be long?"

He had not gone far before he found a place that suited him. A luxuriant patch of ferns growing out of a carpet of moss, bordered on every side with tall brushwood, while overhead giant fir-trees sighed and moaned in the evening breeze, made a perfect arbour of quiet and repose. Pressing down the yielding ferns, he had soon a bed soft as he could desire, while a mossy bank made a pillow grateful as a kiss of love to his aching head and burning cheek.

"I'll be comfortable 'ere till the Lord comes," he said, stretching out his weary limbs. I wonder if He'll bring Nelly wi' Him?"

Then he closed his eyes and waited. Above him the fir-branches swayed gently in the soft evening breeze, and from far away came the subdued plash of falling water. It was very strange and solemn, but soothing and restful withal.

The pangs of hunger abated, too, after he had rested a while, and his head ceased to ache, while the wind in the trees sounded like an evening lullaby, and brought back to him a vague and misty recollection of his mother rocking him to sleep on her lap, in the years long, long ago.

Then the music seemed to come from farther and farther away, till it ceased altogether, and once more Benny slept. And there in the solemn wood we will leave him for a while to the mercy and care that are infinite.

CHAPTER XIX

The Border Land

For since Thy hand hath led me here,
And I have seen the border land, –
Seen the dark river flowing near,
Stood on its bank as now I stand, –
There has been nothing to alarm
My trembling soul; why should I fear?
For since encircled by Thy arm,
I never felt Thee half so near.

JOE Wrag was in great trouble when he heard of Benny's misfortune. Granny was the first to make him acquainted with the fact that something was wrong. Benny had been in the habit of returning earlier on a Saturday evening since he had been with Mr. Lawrence than on any other day of the week, and when that evening wore away and deepened into night, and Benny did not come, granny got very much concerned, fearing some accident had befallen him; and so she remained rocking herself in her chair, and listening in vain for his footfall all through the night. And when morning came she hurried away, old as she was, to Joe's house, in the hope that he would be able to give her some information as to Benny's whereabouts.

Joe was thunderstruck at sight of Betty so early on a Sunday morning, and her eager question, "Dost a' knaw where the boy is, Joe?" did not help to mend matters. For a few moments Joe's power of utterance seemed to have left him altogether, then he stammered forth

"Ain't he home, Betty?"

"Nae, Joe; I's never seen 'im sin yester morn!"

Joe looked thoughtful, for he had no reply to this, and Betty sat down in a chair, evidently exhausted.

After a while Betty got up to go. "I mun be a-goin'," she said, "he may a-got home by now."

Towards evening Joe called at Tempest Court, but nothing had been heard of the wanderer. The night that followed was one of the longest Joe had ever known, and as soon as he was released from his watch in the morning he went at once to Mr. Lawrence's office.

"Is the maaster in?" he said, addressing one of the clerks.

"No, my good man," was the reply; "he will not be down for an hour yet. Could you call again?"

"Mebbe you'll do as weel," said Joe, scratching his head. "Can yer tell me wot's become o' the boy Benny?"

"Oh, yes," said the clerk, smiling complacently, "he's where he ought to have been long ago."

"Where's that?" said Joe.

"In prison, sir!"

"In prison?" in a tone of bewilderment.

"Even so," with a bland smile.

"I can't say as 'ow I hunderstand," Joe stammered out.

"Very likely," said the clerk, "so I will inform you that Mr. Lawrence, having his suspicions aroused, placed a five-pound note on his desk, and then set a watch – "

"Well?" said Joe, eager yet fearing to hear the rest.

"Well," continued the clerk, "this young friend of yours, who seems to have been an old hand at the work, was seen coolly to take the money. But when charged with the theft, a few minutes after, he stoutly denied all knowledge of the

162

circumstance; but Mr. Lawrence was determined to stand no nonsense, and had him at once marched off to the lock-up."

For a moment Joe looked at the clerk in silence, then, without a word, walked out of the office. When he told granny, she was at first indignant. "To think that she, a honest woman, 'ad been a-'arbouring a thief all these months!" But Joe soon talked her into a better frame of mind, and it was then that she promised him that if the prodigal ever came back again she would not turn him away.

When Joe read in the paper on Wednesday morning that Benny was acquitted, his delight knew no bounds. He accepted the fact as almost proof positive that Benny was innocent, and went at once to tell granny the news.

He found the old woman crying over Benny's letter, with the eighteenpence lying in her lap. When Joe came in she handed him the letter without a word. Joe blew his nose violently several times during its perusal, then laid it down on the table, and walked to the door to hide his emotion. It was several moments before he could command himself sufficiently to speak, then he blurted out –

"The poor parsecuted bairn mun be found somehow, Betty, an' 'ere's off to sairch. Good mornin', Betty."

And before the old woman could reply he was gone.

During the next three days Joe had but little sleep. He tramped the town in every direction, in the hope that he might glean some tidings of the poor lost lad; but his labour was in vain, and each evening when he returned to his hut it was with a sadly diminished hope of ever finding the boy again.

On the evening that Benny, hungry and forsaken, lay down in the wood to sleep, Joe felt his heart drawn out in prayer in such a manner as he had never before experienced. Nearly the whole of the night he spent upon

163

his knees. Now, and then he got up and walked out into the silent street, and gazed for a few moments up into the starlit sky. Then he would return to his hut again and pray more fervently than ever. He had returned from his search that evening utterly cast down, feeling that the only resource left to him was prayer. He knew not whether the boy was living or dead. He could hardly think the latter; and yet if he were alive, who could tell what he was suffering? Who but God? To God then he would go and plead for the outcast boy, and who should tell whether God might not regard his prayer and send help and deliverance to the child? Thus hour after hour he prayed on, and when the light of the morning crept up into the eastern sky, he rose from his knees comforted.

Were Joe Wrag's prayers answered? No doubt they were. Not in the way, perhaps, that Joe would have liked best, and yet in the best way for all that. God does not always give us in answer to our prayers what *we* think best, but what *He* thinks best. To weary, worn-out Benny God gave sleep, deep, dreamless, and refreshing, and in the morning he awoke to the song of birds and to the rustle of a thousand leaves. The music sounded very sweet to Benny's ears, but it was not the music of heaven, as he had hoped it would be. He had waited there in the solemn wood for the coming of the Lord, but He had not come. Heaven seemed farther away from him than ever this morning, and earth was painfully real. He felt himself too weak to stir at first, so he lay still, occasionally opening his eyes to watch the slanting sunbeams play among the tangled foliage, and light up the dewdrops that trembled on every leaf.

His head was hot and heavy, and his eyes ached when he kept them open long, and the pangs of hunger were coming on again. What should he do? He lay for a long time trying

164

to think, but his thoughts whirled and twisted like snowflakes in a storm.

"P'raps I kin get on a little furder if I tries," he said to himself at length, and suiting the action to the words, he rose from his ferny bed and staggered out of the wood. He had scarcely strength left to get over the gate, but he managed it at length, and then fell down exhausted by the roadside.

How long he lay there he never knew; but he was aroused at length by the lumbering of some kind of vehicle coming towards him along the road, and by the shrill whistling of the driver.

Nearer and nearer came the vehicle, and then stopped just opposite him. Benny looked up and saw a shock-headed, overgrown lad, standing in what seemed an empty cart, staring at him with a look of wonder in his great round eyes.

Benny had reached a stage of exhaustion which made him indifferent to almost everything, so he only blinked at the boy, and then dropped his head again on the grass.

"Art a tired?" said the boy at length.

"Ay," said Benny, without opening his eyes.

"Wilt a 'ave a lift? "

"What's a lift?"

"A ride, then, if it's properer."

"Ay, I'll ride; but 'ow's I to get in?"

"Oh, aisy 'nough," said young Giles, jumping out of the cart and lifting Benny in as if he had been an infant.

"Golly," said Benny, coming out with his once favourite expression, "you're mighty strong!"

"Strong? You should see me lift a bag o' corn! Now, Dobbin," to the horse. "Gee, meth-a-way," and the horse moved on at what seemed a stereotyped pace.

"'Ave a turmut?" said the boy at length.

"What's a turmut?"

165

"Lor, now," laughed the boy, "you must be green not to know what a turmut is." And he untied the mouth of one of several bags lying at the bottom of the cart, and took out two, and by the aid of a large clasp-knife had both peeled in a 'jiffey'.

Putting his teeth into one, he handed the other to Benny, who readily followed his example, and thought he had never tasted anything more delicious.

By the time our hero had finished his turnip they had reached a small village, and Benny was able to get out of the cart unaided. Here were houses at last. Perhaps he might get work here; he would try, at any rate. And try he did; but it was discouraging work.

At many of the houses the door was slammed in his face in answer to his inquiry. At a few places the person addressed condescended to ask Benny where he came from, and when he replied "from Liverpool," he was told to be off about his business, as they wanted no thieves nor pickpockets in their employ."

One kind-looking old gentleman asked Benny what he could do.

"Anything a'most," was the prompt reply.

"You're too clever by a long way," laughed the old man; "but let's perticlerise a bit. Can you spud thistles?"

Benny looked bewildered. He knew nothing about "spuds" or "thistles," so he shook his head in reply.

"Canst a whet a scythe?"

Another shake of the head.

"Take out arter the mowers?"

"No."

"Dibbel tates?"

"I don't know."

"Humph. Canst a milk?"

"I ken drink it, if that's wot you mean," said Benny.

"Ha! ha! Mary," raising his voice, "fotch the lad a mug o' milk." And in a few moments a stout red-armed girl brought Benny a pint mug, brimful of rich new milk.

"Ay, ay," said the old man, "I see thee canst do thy part in that direction weel eno'. Have another?"

"No, thank you."

"Humph. I fear thee'rt no 'count in the country, lad."

"But I could larn," said Benny.

"Yes, yes, that's true; thee'rt a sharp boy. I shouldn't wonder if thee couldn't get a job at t' next village."

"How far?" said Benny.

"Short o' two mile, I should say."

"Thank you." And once more Benny set off on the tramp. It was scarcely noon, and the day was melting hot. Outside the village the sun's rays beat down pitilessly on his head, and made him feel sick and giddy. All the trees were on the wrong side of the road, and he looked in vain for a shady spot along the dusty highway. Still on he tramped, with fast failing strength. A little way before him he saw a farmhouse, with trees growing around it. "If I can only reach that," he thought, "I'll rest a while." Nearer and nearer, but how strangely everything was swimming around him, and what a curious mist was gathering before his eyes!

Ah, there is the sound of voices; a group of haymakers just inside the gate getting their dinner in the shadow of a tree. Was help at hand? He did not know. Gathering up all his strength, he staggered towards them, stretched out his hand blindly, for the mist had deepened before his eyes, then lifted his hands to his temples, as if struck with sudden pain, reeled, and fell senseless to the ground.

In a moment a woman raised him from the ground, and supported his head against her knee, while the men crowded round with wondering faces. Then Farmer Fisher came up with the question, "What's to do?" and the haymakers stood aside, that he might see for himself.

"The boy's dead," said the farmer, with just a little shake in his voice.

"No," said the woman, "he's not dead, his heart beats still."

"Go and call the missus, then, quick."

Then one of the men started for the farmhouse.

Mrs. Fisher was a gentle, kind-hearted woman at all times, especially to children, and just now she was particularly so, for a month had not elapsed since she had laid one of her own children, a boy of about Benny's age, in the silent grave. And when she caught sight of Benny's white suffering face, her heart went out to him instantly.

"Take him into the house, John," she said to her husband, the tears starting in her eyes, "and send for the doctor at once."

So without further ado Benny was carried into the house, stripped of his dirty and ragged attire, put into a warm bath, and then laid gently in a clean soft bed, in a cool pleasant room. Once only he opened his eyes, looked around him with a bewildered air, then relapsed again into unconsciousness.

The doctor, who arrived toward evening, pronounced it a very bad case, ordered port wine to be poured down his throat in small quantities during the night, and promised to call again next day.

"Will he live?" was Mrs, Fisher's anxious question.

"Fear not," said the doctor: "want, exposure, and I fear also sunstroke, have done their work. Whoever the little fellow belongs to, he's had a hard time of it, and to such death should not be unwelcome."

During the next day Benny was conscious at brief intervals, but he lay so perfectly still, with half-closed eyes, that they hardly knew at times whether he was alive or dead. His face was as white as the pillow on which he lay, and his breathing all but imperceptible. The doctor shook his head when he came, but held out no hope of recovery.

So that summer Sabbath passed away, and Monday came and went, and Tuesday followed in the track, and Wednesday dawned, and still Benny's life trembled in the balance. The doctor said there was no perceptible increase of strength, while the pulse, if anything, was weaker. Hence, without some great change, he thought the boy would not live many hours longer.

Outside the birds twittered in the trees, and the songs of the haymakers floated on the still summer air; but within, in a darkened room, little Benny to all appearance lay dying. He had reached the border land, and was standing on the river's brink. On the other side of the stream was the everlasting home, where his Nelly dwelt, and where hunger and weariness and pain could never come. Why did he linger, when he wanted so much to cross and be at rest for ever?

He had no fear, and to the onlookers it seemed easy dying. No sigh or moan escaped his lips; he lay as still as the dead.

The day waned at length and darkened into night, and Mrs. Fisher and one of the servants remained up to watch by the little invalid. It was about midnight when they observed a change come over him. The brow contracted as if in pain, the wasted fingers plucked at the clothes, and the breathing became heavy and irregular.

Mrs. Fisher ran to her husband's room and summoned him at once to Benny's bedside. John Fisher was a kind man, and needed no second bidding. With a gentle hand he wiped away the big drops that were gathering on the little sufferer's brow; then turning to his wife, he said, "Do you think you had better stay, love? I think he is dying."

"No, no!" she said, "I cannot see him die." Then, after a pause, she sobbed, "Let me know when it is over, John," and hurried from the room.

CHAPTER XX

Life at the Farm

Source of my life's refreshing springs,
Whose presence in my heart sustains me,
Thy love appoints me pleasant things,
Thy mercy orders all that pains me.

Well may Thine own beloved, who see
In all their lot their Father's pleasure,
Bear loss of all they love, save Thee –
Their living, everlasting treasure.

Waring

MRS. FISHER waited anxiously in an adjoining room for the coming of her husband to tell her that Benny was no more. She could not go back into the sick-room, she dared not see the child die. It was only such a short time ago she held her own dying Rob in her arms while he gasped out his little life, and the wound in her heart was not healed yet: she fancied it never would be. The sick child in the next room, that she had taken to her heart, had opened it afresh, and she felt that to see the little fellow struggling in the agonies of death would be more than her nerves could bear. And so she waited while the moments dragged slowly along.

"How tenaciously the child clings to life!" she said to

171

herself as she paced restlessly up and down the room. Still her husband came not.

"Can he be fighting death all this while?" she said; "I hope the little spirit will be released soon." Then she fell upon her knees and prayed – prayed long and earnestly that, if it were the Lord's will, the boy that had been thrown upon their care might have a speedy and sweet release from the burden of the flesh.

It seemed long since she had left the sick-room, and still the moments travelled slowly on.

"It cannot be much longer," she said; then a step on the landing made her look up anxiously, and her husband came quickly into the room.

"Come this way, Mary," he said, without waiting for her to speak.

"Is it all over?" she questioned, looking up into his face.

"No, I can't understand it at all: the lad seems better, though he's evidently wrong in his head."

Without further remark, she went at once to the bedside, and laid her hand gently upon his forehead. Benny opened his eyes slowly, and raised them to her face, then tried to speak, but only a faint whisper escaped his lips.

"What do you say, poor boy?" said Mrs. Fisher kindly, bending down her ear to listen.

"May I see Nelly, please?" he whispered.

"Who is Nelly?" she replied.

"Nelly is my sister; may I not see her?" in the same faint whisper.

"Where is your sister, my boy?" said Mrs. Fisher looking a little perplexed.

"Nelly's in heaven," he said. "This is heaven, ain't it?"

"No, my boy, this is not heaven," she replied.

"Oh, I thought it wur," he said, closing his eyes with a

172

look of pain. And Mrs. Fisher's eyes became moist, as she saw the big tears stealing out under the lashes, and rolling slowly down the pale wasted cheeks.

After a while Benny fell into a sound sleep, from which he did not awake till morning. When the doctor came next day he rubbed his hands with glee.

"Never had but one case before to equal it!" he said, "but it's wonderful what children will pull through: just as you think they are going right over the precipice, they turn round, and coolly walk back into health."

"Do you think he will get better?" said Mrs. Fisher.

"More likely than not," was the reply: "the tide has turned, evidently. He had reached the crisis when you thought he was dying last night, and instead of kicking the beam, why, here he is ever so much better."

From that day Benny got better. Not rapidly; no, it was a slow coming back to health; still, he did get better. Day by day he gathered strength, though scarcely perceptible at times. The doctor rather wondered at this, for he expected his recovery to be much more rapid. But the secret lay in the fact that Benny did not want to get better. And one day, about a week after the time of which we have spoken, he positively refused to take his medicine.

"But it is to make you better," said Mrs. Fisher gently.

"But I dunna want to get better," said Benny; "I wants to go to heaven."

"But you should be willing to wait the Lord's time, Benny."

"I's waited so long," he said fretfully, "that I's tired of waitin'."

"But it's wrong to murmur at what is God's will, Benny."

"Are it?" he said. "I didn't know, but I's very tired."

"But you'll get rested after a while, if you'll be patient."

"Ah, then," he said, with a sigh, "I mun try, I s'pose."

But in spite of Benny's anxiety to die, health and strength came back to him day by day, and one beautiful July Sabbath afternoon he was dressed, for the first time, in a suit of dead Rob's clothes, and carried into another room, and placed in an easy chair by the window, that he might feast his eyes on the beautiful landscape that stretched out before him. Benny submitted to the process without speaking a word, for he was still very weak; but after he had recovered himself a little, he looked curiously at the clothes in which he was enveloped, as if not at all certain of his identity.

"I reckon I's not Benny Bates," he said at length.

"Oh, yes, you are," said Mrs. Fisher, who had been watching him with an amused smile upon her face.

"Then," he said, looking up, "these is not my togs."

"No; but I think I'll give them to you, Benny."

"Whew!" lifting his eyebrows.

Then he began to search carefully all the pockets; that done, he lifted his white scared face to Mrs. Fisher, and said, "Where's the bob, please?"

"Where's what?"

"The shillin'."

"What shilling?"

"The one the angel gived me. Ain't yer seen it?"

"No; where was it?"

"In the linen' of my wesket."

"Oh, then, perhaps we can find it."

"Oh, yes, do, please; I wouldna lose that bob for a hunderd poun'."

"A hundred pounds is a lot of money, Benny."

"Don't care; don't you see? an angel gived it to me."

"An angel, Benny?"

"Ay, an angel, a real one; but if you'll find the bob, I'll tell

174

yer all 'bout it."

After some searching the shilling was found, and Benny, as good as his word, told Mrs. Fisher the story connected with it. In fact, he would, now that the ice was broken, have told that day all the story of his life, but Mrs. Fisher insisted that it would tire him too much, and that she would hear it some other day.

So day after day as he sat by the window, with the soft summer breeze fanning his brow, and with the songs of the birds in his ears, he told the story that we have written. Told of his father's cruelty, of Joe Wrag's friendship, and of his sister's love – told of his sorrow and loss, his hunger and despair, and of the angel that came to him in his hour of need – told of his success in Mr. Lawrence's office, of his thirst for knowledge, and of the bright hopes he cherished for the future. And he told her, too of the charge of theft, of his imprisonment and temptation, of his release and resolve, of his fierce battle with hunger and want; and how, to be out of the reach of temptation, he had wandered away into the country until, worn out with hunger and fatigue, he lay down to die.

And while Mrs. Fisher listened, she felt thankful that she had been able to befriend the homeless boy. Benny was winning his way to her motherly heart in a wonderful manner, and was helping to fill the gap caused by the death of little Rob. And could she have had her own way, she would have adopted him as her own, and sent him to school when he was strong enough, with Harry and George. But Benny's independent spirit would not hear of it. He would stay at Scout Farm if he might be permitted to earn his own living; but if they could not find employment for him he must go out into the great world once more, and try over again to earn, by some means, his daily bread. So it was

175

settled at length that he should stay, and learn to be a farmer; and then Benny grew strong rapidly, and ere the sunny September days passed away, he was out in the breezy fields helping to gather in the late harvest, and trying to make himself useful in every possible way. He was willing, nay, anxious to learn, and the work was by no means difficult. For the first few weeks he was very tired when evening came, but the fresh air gave him an appetite, and the work developed his muscles, and life once more became to him a joy.

He very soon got to know what to do without being told. He would tie up the cattle in the evening as if he had been used to a farm all his life; groom the horses as if he and they were old acquaintances; and feed the calves with all the dispatch of an old hand at the work. Mr. Fisher was delighted with him; "a handier little chap," he declared, "he had never come across." And instead of being in the way, as Mrs. Fisher feared he would be, he soon made himself necessary to them.

When winter came, with its long dreary evenings, he found a new source of pleasure, and that was a night school. It was Mrs. Fisher – to whom he had spoken of his thirst for knowledge – that persuaded him to attend. She knew he would not only derive pleasure, but profit. Benny was considerably puzzled at first as to what a "night school" was like; but he soon discovered its purpose, and night after night, through wind and rain, he plodded along the dark country lane to the neighbouring village of Scoutleigh, eager to improve his mind and add to his small store of knowledge. Never had a village schoolmaster a more diligent pupil than he, and rarely one that improved more rapidly.

Nor did he forget in the summer that followed what he had learnt during the winter. There were books in Mr. Fisher's house, to which he had free access, for though on the farm he worked side by side with the hired servants, in the house he was treated as one of the family; and when the day's work was done, he found in his books his most congenial companions. And so he grew in body and mind, and thanked God in his heart for the haven he had found at last.

Time passed quickly at Scout Farm. There was always so much to be done that he had little time to brood over the past, or sigh over "what might have been." Occasionally he longed for the busy life of the town he had left, but the feeling was only momentary. On the whole he was pleased with the life he was living, and though he saw no prospect of ever realising the dreams that once he cherished, yet he tried to be content. So the weeks passed away, and lengthened into months, and the months lengthened into years, almost unconsciously to Benny. He found himself growing into a man almost against his will.

*****

Six years passed away, and Benny had grown almost out of recognition. No one would have thought that the tall, handsome young fellow that did so large a share of the work at Scout Farm, was the pale and famished child that dragged himself along the dusty highway six years before. He used to laugh sometimes when reminded of the past, and say that he was an example of what hard work, fresh air, and good food could accomplish. Mr. Fisher was almost as proud of him as if he had been his own son, and never seemed tired of declaring that "Ben Bates could swing a scythe, shear a sheep, plough a furrow, build a corn-stack, or thatch a hay-rick equal to any man for ten miles round." Nor was John Fisher the only man that sang Benny's praises. The superintendent of the Methodist Sunday-school at Scoutleigh averred that Benny was the most punctual, diligent, and successful teacher he had.

Benny always declared, however, that he learnt more than he ever taught. Up to the time that he commenced to teach, he had looked upon religion as stern, cold duty, and as that only; a question simply of doing or not doing. It is true that he heard occasionally sermons on the subject of experimental religion, but he thought it was only a way the preachers had of expressing themselves. He had no doubt that he was a Christian. He had been trying to be one ever since the death of his little Nell; he said his prayers regularly, and always tried to do his duty; and he asked himself what more could he do. Yet as he studied the New Testament carefully week by week, in order that he might instruct his class of boys, he became slowly conscious of the fact that feelings and experiences were hinted at in that Book of books that he was a stranger to. What did he know about that "peace that passeth understanding," or of "rejoicing with joy unspeakable"? Was his life "hid with Christ in God," and was he certain what was meant by "holding communion with God and fellowship with Christ"? He now began to pay more attention to the sermons that were preached, and to the hymns that were sung. One Sunday morning he stopped singing at the verse.

> "Jesus, Thine all-victorious love
> Shed in my heart abroad,
> Then shall my feet no longer rove,
> Rooted and fixed in God."

"What did it mean?" he asked himself, "this love shed abroad in the heart, inspiring the life, beautifying the character? Was religion as much a matter of love as of duty?" He heard nothing of the lesson that was read; but when the congregation stood up to sing again he was all attention. Slowly the words rang out, and filled the little sanctuary.

"Give me the faith which can remove
And sink the mountain to a plain;
Give me the child-like praying love
Which longs to build Thy house again;
Thy love, let it my heart o'erpower,
And all my simple soul devour.

"Enlarge, inflame, and fill my heart
With boundless charity divine!
So shall I all my strength exert,
And love them with a zeal like Thine,
And lead them to Thy open side,
The sheep for whom the Shepherd died."

That hymn for the rest of the day became the burden of his prayer, and for many days after, though when the answer came, or how, Benny never knew. That it did come he had no doubt, for he discovered that religion was no longer the cold formal thing he had once imagined it to be, but a warm living something that filled his whole life. Duty now became a joy, because love inspired it. Loving God, he loved His service and loved His people; and at last he understood the words of the Master, "My meat is to do the will of Him that sent Me, and to finish His work."

I do not know that anyone saw any change in Benny's life, except perhaps the superintendent of the school. He taught from henceforth as if his whole heart and soul were in the work; duty was no longer irksome, but a delight, and when some of the boys of his class were raised to a higher one, he went out into the village and got other boys to take their places. Thus in earnest Christian work he spent his Sabbath days; and on the Monday morning he would start out into the fields with a light heart, feeling all the happier and stronger for doing the Master's work on the previous day.

For many months nothing had happened to disturb the quiet and peaceful lives that were lived at Scout Farm. Harry and George were at college, one studying to be a doctor, the other to be a solicitor. Winnie, the baby – born since Benny came to the farm – had grown into a bonny little creature, the pet of all the household; and Mr. and Mrs. Fisher were as contented with their lot as two people could be, and wanted no change of any kind. Benny was a little restless at times, but on the whole was happy. But this quiet life could not be lived always, and soon afterwards a circumstance transpired which was destined to affect Benny's future in a way that he had no conception of. What that circumstance was shall be told in another chapter.

CHAPTER XXI

An Accident

The sea of fortune doth not ever flow,
She draws her favours to the lowest ebb.
Her tides have equal time to come and go,
Her looms doth weave the fine and coarsest web.
No joy so great, but runneth to an end,
No hap so hard but may in time amend.

Southwell

NOT far from Scout Farm were several gentlemen's residences, occupied chiefly by Manchester merchants, who travelled to and from the city morning and evening by rail. One of the largest of these residences, and also the farthest away from Scoutleigh Road Station, was occupied by a Mr. Munroe, who was reputed to be a man of great wealth, and also of great liberality. In consequence of the distance of Mr. Munroe's house from the station, his coachman used to drive him to Scoutleigh Road in the morning and fetch him in the evening, sometimes taking Mrs. Munroe, or one of the children, at the same time.

Mrs. Munroe was the only sister of Mr. Lawrence, of Liverpool, Benny's former master, and, at the time to which we refer, Eva Lawrence was spending a few weeks at Brooklands with her uncle and aunt. Little did our hero think, as he sometimes looked across the valley at Mr.

Munroe's house, almost hidden by trees, that his 'angel' was staying there. It was doubtless well for him that he did not know. He would have been impatient to look once more upon the face of the maiden that, next to his sister Nelly, had been the brightest vision of his life. He still kept the shilling that she had given him, and often when alone he would take it out of his purse and look at it, and wonder what had become of the little girl that befriended him in his hour of need, and would almost long for one more sight of her angel face.

It was at such times as these that Benny grew restless, and pined for the bustle of Liverpool streets, and for the sight of old faces, that day by day were fading from his memory. Yet he never seriously entertained the idea of going back. There were only Joe and granny, and Mr. Lawrence and Eva, that he cared to see, but that they would care to see him was very doubtful, and he could not go back to be looked at with suspicion. And not only so: he believed that he was where God intended him to be. He had a home, and a good one, among friends who believed in his honesty and treated him with kindness. And even yet, had he been disposed to pay a visit to his old haunts, he had no time. He was fully employed every day of the week, and every season of the year brought its appointed work. The days were so short in winter that he had always his hands full, and sometimes more than he could do. And spring was always a busy time: the lambs had to be attended to; fences had to be repaired; and so many "crops" had to be got in, that hay harvest came upon them frequently before they were ready. Then huge fields of turnips and mangolds and potatoes had to be hoed, and ere that was done the fields were white unto the harvest. Then came sheep-shearing and ploughing land for next year's wheat crop, and potato digging, and half a dozen other things, that allowed him no time for idleness, and it was well for Benny that it was so. He had no time to mope or to waste in useless regrets.

One evening he had to pass Brooklands on his way to a neighbouring farm. The day had been beautifully fine – a real June day, people said; a few people complained that it had been too hot about noon, but as the day declined a fresh breeze had sprung up, that made the evening deliciously cool. Benny enjoyed few things more than a saunter across the fields during a summer's evening. And this evening he was just in the mood to enjoy the song of birds, and the scent of apple blossom and new-mown hay. It wanted several hours yet of sundown, so he sauntered on very leisurely, and paused when near Mr. Munroe's house, arrested by the sound of laughter. Not far from where he stood three or four young ladies were engaged in a game of archery, and as he could not be seen by them, he waited a while to watch them. He did not know that one of those fair maidens was Eva Lawrence; how should he know? She was a little girl when he saw her last, now she was just blooming into womanhood. The beauty, of which her early life gave promise, was now more than realised. But had Eva Lawrence been plain of feature, she would still have been beautiful in the eyes of those who knew her well. Hers was a beautiful life, and people did not wonder that it was mirrored in a lovely face. It was a picture that would have pleased an artist's eye on which Benny gazed, and their rippling laughter formed a pleasant accompaniment to the rustling of the leaves and the music of the brook that murmured down the glen. But as Benny gazed at the picture he only saw one face, that of Eva Lawrence. He thought he had never seen the face before, and yet it affected him strangely. It seemed to bring back to him some half-forgotten dream. What was it that it reminded him of? He could not tell; whatever it might be, it eluded his grasp. Like the snatch of a forgotten song it came and went, leaving nothing definite upon the mind.

An hour later he returned by another way across the glen or ravine (adown which the brook babbled) by a narrow bridge with low parapets, and turned a sudden corner down the lane towards Scout Farm. For a moment he paused and remarked to himself, "This is a dangerous corner; I wonder Mr. Munroe does not alter it; and that bridge too, it is altogether too narrow. If I drove this way as often as he does, I would pull down that antiquated structure, and build a good wide bridge with a high wall on either side;" and, having given expression to an opinion that he had expressed a hundred times before, he turned on his heel and quietly pursued his way. He had not gone many yards, however, before he heard a great hue and cry, and, looking down the lane, he saw that Mr. Munroe's horse had taken fright, and was rushing towards him at headlong speed. The coachman, who had been riding behind, had coolly dropped himself down on the road, and stood staring after the flying carriage in blank astonishment, and shouting at the top of his voice. Benny saw that Mr. Munroe was trying in vain to check the mad gallop of the horse, and he saw also that the young lady whose face had attracted him so strangely before was sitting by his side, pale and motionless. Here and there people rushed out from the fields into the road and held up their hands or hoes, but always retreated after a few frantic gesticulations in time for the affrighted steed to pass. Instantly Benny thought of the sharp corner and the narrow bridge over the deep ravine. If the road had been straight, the wisest course would have been to have given the horse rein, and let it tire itself out. But as it was, the horse must

184

be stopped before it reached the bridge, or almost certain death would be the fate of Mr. Munroe and his niece. He had little time to think, but he knew that to attempt to stop the horse would be attended with considerable risk to himself. If he failed to grasp the bridle the horse and carriage would go over him, in all probability killing him on the spot; but he had no time to debate the question, the startled horse was full upon him. In an instant he dashed at the bridle and caught it, the end of the shaft striking him on the arm at the same moment, almost causing him to let go his hold, but he held tight. For a dozen yards the horse dragged him along the road; then he succeeded in getting it on its knees with its nose against a hedge, and Mr. Munroe and Eva alighted in perfect safety. By this time, however, a number of people had gathered round, the coachman amongst the rest, who at once took charge of the horse, and Benny slunk away as quietly as possible, and made his way along the road as fast as he was able. Mr. Munroe, however, seeing his intentions, followed him at once.

"Come, come, my young friend," he said; "I cannot let you go without thanking you for your noble act."

"Do not mention it, sir," said Benny, with an effort, turning pale at the same time.

"I would be ungrateful indeed," said Mr. Munroe, "were I not to mention it. No, I shall never forget that to your heroism my niece and myself owe our lives."

"I am very thankful if I have been of service to you," said Benny; "but I could not have acted otherwise, so please – "

But he did not finish the sentence: setting his teeth together, as if in pain, he staggered towards a seat by the hedge.

Instantly Mr. Munroe sprang towards him, exclaiming, "You're hurt, I'm sure you are; tell me what's the matter."

"My arm is broken, that is all," said Benny, with a poor attempt at a smile; then everything began to spin around him in a very bewildering manner, and he could never exactly recollect what happened after. He always carried with him, however, a lively recollection of the process of bone-setting, which he afterwards underwent, and of the sleepless night that followed.

Next morning Mr. Munroe came to Scout Farm and sat with Benny for half an hour, chatting about things in general, and before he left he thanked him again in the warmest terms for his bravery, and made him promise to visit Brooklands as soon as he was able, stating that Mrs. Munroe was very anxious to see him, as were also his daughters and niece, especially the latter, who wanted to thank him personally for saving her life.

Benny blushed at first and begged to be excused, but Mr. Munroe would not hear of it. So Benny reluctantly consented at last to endure the martyrdom (to him) of being introduced to the fine ladies at the big house, and in his heart wished he was well out of it all. He felt sure that he should look silly and make a hole in his manners, for he had never been used to grand people; and what would be the proper thing to say when they thanked him he had not the remotest idea.

"Well, Ben Bates," he said to himself when Mr. Munroe had left the room, "you're in for it now, and no mistake. Here's a pretty kettle of fish for you, my lad, and you've to see to it that you don't go and make a fool of yourself. A lot you know about etiquette and drawing-room manners; and won't you do the graceful before the ladies? Oh, dear, dear!"

And he laughed till the tears ran down his face, spite the pain in his arm.

"I think I see you going through the introduction, my lad,

trying to do the thing proper as if you knew how, and only succeeding in making yourself look silly. And won't the ladies giggle after you're gone!"

Then Benny looked serious, and after a long pause he went on again: "Look here, Ben Bates: do you think you are a downright fool, or do you think you have just a few grains of common sense? For, unless you're a born natural, you'll put on no airs at the big house; but you'll just be yourself, remember, and not ape anybody else; you profess a great hatred of sham, then don't be a sham yourself, and make yourself look ridiculous. Remember what you are, Ben Bates; and remember, too, that you've got nothing to be ashamed of."

Then, after another pause: "I wish I was well out of this job, notwithstanding. I hate to be thanked. I wonder, by-the-bye, who that young lady is? How her face reminds me of something, something in the old life, but what I cannot make out. How strange everything seems! I fancy sometimes I must have lived here always, and dreamed all the rest. But no, Nelly was real, and that shilling was real. Ah! I wonder what's become of her." And a far-away look came into his eyes, as if he were back again in the old life of mingled joy and pain.

Meanwhile Mr. Munroe was out in the yard talking with Mr. Fisher.

"A fine young fellow that of yours, Mr. Fisher," was his first greeting.

"Yes," said the farmer; "I'd back him against any young man his age for ten miles round."

"An adopted son of yours, I suppose?"

"Well, no, not exactly," replied Mr. Fisher.

"Beg pardon, I thought you had adopted him."

"Well, perhaps you are not far wrong either. You see, he

came to us five or six years agone, a poor little famished, wizened creature. It was a sweltering hot day too, and he had walked all the day from Liverpool, sleeping at nights by the roadside, and by the time he got here – or rather, he didn't get here – our folks were making hay in the home close, and he just got inside the gate, and dropped down in a fit, or something of the sort. Well, he was completely done up; the doctor never thought he would come round again, but he did, and you see what a fine fellow he's grown to."

"Yes, indeed! And so he has lived with you ever since?"

"Ever since. My wife says she believes the Lord directed him here. Any way, the boy was a great comfort to her, for we'd only just buried our little Rob, and he seemed to fill up the gap a bit, you see."

"I suppose you find him very handy about the farm now, Mr. Fisher?"

"Handy? I tell you, there isn't his equal for miles around. He took to the farm as natural as a duck takes to the water. In fact, the plucky little dog said he wouldn't stay to be a burden to us, and he never has been. In fact, if we came to square accounts, I fancy that I should find that I was considerably in his debt."

"And you find him perfectly trustworthy?"

"He's as honest as the daylight, sir, and as good as gold. Why, I'd trust him with my life, and so would the missus. She thinks a sight of him, I can assure you."

"I do not wonder at it, Mr. Fisher; he's a brave young fellow, and deserves notice and help – if he needed it."

"Brave? Well, you've said just right in that, Mr. Munroe; he's as brave as a lion. I don't think the young dog knows what fear is. I expect it'll be getting him into trouble some of these days. But then, bless you, on the other hand, he's as gentle as a woman, and the very soul of kindness. I believe the young scamp would give away the last copper he had, if he saw someone he fancied wanted it more than himself."

"Indeed!" said Mr. Munroe, feeling rather amused at Mr. Fisher's enthusiasm. "It is not often you see people possessing so many good qualities."

"Good! Well, you've hit it again, the lad is good; and yet, mark you, he ain't none of the goody-goody sort either. Why, bless you, he's as full of fun and frolic as an egg is full of meat. You should just see the carryings on we have here when the lads are home from school. I laugh sometimes fit to kill myself, and yet feel as mad as a sheep at 'em, for they give me no peace of my life."

"Well, we cannot expect the young folks to be as sedate and steady-going as we older people, Mr. Fisher."

"That's what my wife says, sir; she says it's as natural for the lads to play as it is for the kittens, and that it's quite as harmless, and I don't think she's far wrong. In fact, I generally give in to her; she's had a sight better education than ever I had, so she ought to know better."

"Ah, speaking about education, Mr. Fisher, what sort of education has this young man had?"

"Well, Mr. Munroe, I confess I'm no judge in matters of that sort. You see, he was never at a day school a day in his life; but for all that he seems to have a natural gift for learning. Our George says he's got on wonderfully; and old Mr. Jones, that keeps the night school yonder at Scoutleigh, says he can't teach him any more."

"Excuse me asking all these questions, Mr. Fisher, but I feel quite interested in the young man. It's but natural I should, since I owe my life to him; and I should like to do something for him, if I could see how it's to be done."

"It's very kind of you, I'm sure, and I can assure you you'll not find me stand in the lad's way. Fact is, I've thought many times of late that he's too good – too well informed, and that kind of thing – to be a farm labourer all his life, and he'd never get enough as a day labourer to become a farmer on his own account."

"Just so; the same thought has occurred to me, but we'll see what can be done. Good morning, Mr. Fisher."

"Good morning, sir, good morning."

And Mr. Fisher went his way to his farm, and Mr. Munroe to the station, to catch the noon train to Manchester.

Benny kept indoors two whole days, and declared that they were two of the longest days of his life. But on the third morning he was out in the fields again with his arm in a sling. He could not work, so he took a book with him and lay down by a sunny hedge, and read till dinner-time. He would not be treated as an invalid.

"I'm all right but for my game arm," he said to Mrs. Fisher, when she brought him some little delicacy that she had cooked for his special benefit; "and I think I know someone that will enjoy it a great deal more than I should," looking across to baby Winnie, who was eyeing the dish with curious eyes! "At any rate, she shall have a share. Come here, Winnie," he said, turning to the child, "come to Benny."

And the little bit of humanity slipped off her chair in what Benny would have once characterised as "sca'se no time," and came toddling round the table towards him, holding up her little fat dimpled hands, and with eyes brimful of delight.

"Take us up, 'enny," said the little prattler; "Winnie 'oves 'oo very much."

"Easier said than done, you young foxy," said Benny, laughing down upon the child. "Come, mammy," turning to Mrs. Fisher, "lend us a helping hand, and get this young soldier where she wants to be." And soon Benny and baby were eating out of the same dish, and it would have been hard to decide which enjoyed it most.

So day after day passed away, and Benny kept putting off the promised visit to Brooklands. Mrs. Fisher was constantly reminding him of his promise, and yet every day he found some fresh excuse for staying away.

One afternoon, however, about a fortnight after the accident, he announced to Mrs. Fisher that he was going to pay his promised visit to the lions that afternoon.

"That's right, Benny; though I don't think from your own experience that you have any occasion to call the ladies lions," and Mrs. Fisher bent on him a knowing look.

"Right you are, mammy; I believe they are mostly angels after all, and perhaps those at Brooklands will be no exception to the rule."

"I'm sure they will be kind to you, Benny; so you had better be off and get ready."

Half an hour later he came into the sitting-room to Mrs. Fisher, dressed for his visit.

"Now, mammy," he said, "am I presentable?"

"Go away with you," she said, laughing, though casting at the same time an admiring look at the manly young fellow that stood before her, "you'll be as proud as a peacock soon."

"Right you are again. I feel the pride creeping up already. But now for a sight of the angels, so good bye." And off he started to pay a visit that was to be fraught with vastly more important issues than he had any conception of.

CHAPTER XXII

Recognition

"That strain again; it had a dying fall:
Oh, it came o'er my ear like the sweet south
That breathes upon a bank of violets,
Stealing and giving odour."

The Tempest

WHEN our hero reached the bridge that spanned the narrow dell, he paused for a moment and looked over the low parapet at the deep gully that had been worn away by the action of the water, and shuddered as he thought of what would have happened had he failed to grasp the bridle-rein. "I expect this break-neck place will be remedied now," he said, "that a couple of lives have come near being lost over it. If the horse had not been stopped there could not have been the least possible chance of their escape. Well, well, I'm thankful the affair ended in nothing worse than a broken arm."

Passing through the lodge gates, he wended his way slowly along the carriage drive towards the house. High above his head the leafy canopy swayed gently in the summer breeze, making pleasant music, and here and there an industrious bee droned dreamily on leaf and flower. From distant fields the sheep-bells jingled gently, and mingled with the whistling of a ploughboy riding home his tired team, while from a neighbouring farmyard the patient cows lowed lazily while waiting to be milked.

When Benny reached the door of the Munroe mansion, he felt strongly tempted to turn and go back again; but concluding that such an action would be exceedingly foolish, he seized the bell-handle, gave it a vigorous pull, and waited.

"Is Mr. Munroe at home?" he inquired of the servant who opened the door.

"Yes; but he's engaged at present. Will you give me your name?"

"Bates. But never mind, you need not disturb him; another time will do as well."

"I think the master has been expecting you to call," with a glance at Benny's arm.

"Very likely. I said I would call some afternoon." "I'm sure he will see you, then. Come this way, please, into the library."

Benny followed without a word, and soon found himself surrounded on every side with books.

"Oh, my!" he said, "I think I should enjoy spending a fortnight here. I wonder how long it would take me to read all these books, and how much longer to understand them? Ay, that's the rub – understanding and remembering what one does read."

Then he ran his eye along shelf after shelf, reading only the titles.

"I expect I should feel like a boy in a sweet-shop, not knowing which bottle to start with. Ah, Wordsworth!" as his eye caught the name. "I've heard of him. I wonder what the inside is like?"

He must have found something very interesting, for when Mr. Munroe came into the room half an hour later, Benny did not notice his entrance. Mr. Munroe watched him with an amused smile on his face for about five minutes, then said, "I'm glad you've found something to take your fancy, Mr. Bates."

Benny started, and blushed to the roots of his hair, In the first place he thought he was alone, and in the second place it was the first time that he had ever been addressed as "mister".

"I beg pardon," he stammered out at length. "I did not know you were in the room."

"Don't mention it. I'm glad to see that you are fond of books; and I'm glad to see you here."

Benny blushed again, but did not reply.

"I was afraid you were not coming," went on, Mr. Munroe; "but how is your arm?"

"Getting on nicely, thank you; the doctor says it will soon be as right as ever."

"I'm glad to hear it. It's a mercy we were not every one of us killed; but I'm having a new bridge built. I've been *going* to have it done for the last ten years, but kept putting it off; however, they are going to start with the job next week."

"I'm very glad to hear it," said Benny. "It's not safe as it is at present."

"No, no; you're quite right there."

Then there was an awkward pause, and Benny began to feel uncomfortable. Mr. Munroe was the first to speak.

"I wanted to see you here," he said, "to have a little conversation with you about – about – yourself," bringing out the last word with a jerk.

Benny did not know what reply to make to this, so he said nothing.

"I understand you have not always lived in the country?" questioned Mr. Munroe.

"No, sir; I lived in Liverpool till I was twelve or thirteen years of age."

"And how do you like farming?"

"Very well, I think; but, really, I've scarcely thought about it."

"You are not uncomfortable, then?"

"Oh, no! far from it. Mr. and Mrs. Fisher took me in when I was houseless, homeless, friendless, and all but dead, and ever since have treated me with the utmost kindness. I have a better home now than I ever had before in my life, and as for the work I do, I feel that it's but poor compensation for the kindness bestowed upon me."

"You have no wish, then, to be anything different to what you are?"

"I did not say so, sir; but as I have no expectation of being other than what I am, I try to be content."

"Ah, just so; and yet I am told you have paid considerable attention to intellectual pursuits."

"I have tried to make the most of my opportunities for acquiring knowledge. I'm fond of books – very; and knowledge I love for its own sake."

"Well spoken, Mr. Bates. I like to hear a young man talk in that way. You are a good penman, Mr. Jones tells me."

"He has paid me that compliment before, but I am scarcely a judge."

"You understand bookkeeping?"

"A little."

"Double entry?"

"Yes."

"Quick at accounts?"

"I should think not. I have scarcely had sufficient practice."

"I suppose if you stay on the farm there is no prospect of your rising to anything higher than a day labourer?"

"Not much, I fear."

"Well, now, Mr. Bates, I may as well out with it first as last. I am very much pleased with you; I am, indeed. I cannot forget that you saved my life, and the life of my niece; and I am anxious to help you to something better than being a farm labourer if you will let me. Almost anyone can do farm work, and I think you are deserving of something better, because you have educated yourself for it. Now, I shall be glad to take you into my city office, and give you a start in life. I commenced as a clerk at the desk, and what I have accomplished there is no reason why you may not. What do you say, now?"

"I hardly know what to say," said Benny. "I am very much obliged to you for your kind offer, but I would like to talk with Mr. and Mrs. Fisher about the matter before I came to a decision."

"You are quite right, Mr. Bates. Let me know this day week; and now let us go into the drawing-room and see the ladies."

Benny followed Mr. Munroe like one in a dream up a broad flight of stairs, and into a large and luxuriantly furnished room. Then commenced the introduction which he had so much dreaded. He bowed to each one in turn, Mr. Munroe mentioning the name of each person; but Benny never heard a word he said, and he sat down with a feeling of infinite relief, and took up a volume of Milton that was lying on a table near him. Then Miss Munroe came forward with the question, "Are you fond of poetry, Mr. Bates?"

"Yes, very."

"You know Wordsworth, of course.

"No. I ought to be ashamed to say so, but I do not."

And then followed a conversation about poets and authors of various kinds, and Benny soon forgot his shyness, and chatted away with as much freedom as if he had been at Scout Farm.

By-and-bye Eva Lawrence came forward shyly, and with a soft blush tinging neck and face; and Miss Munroe rose and left her and Benny together. It was growing dusk by this time, and she sat with her back to the light, so that Benny could scarcely see her face.

"I am very grateful to you, Mr. Bates," she began in a low voice, "for your bravery in stopping our horse the other night."

Benny started, for something in the voice reminded him again of other days, and he did not reply for a moment; and Eva went on

"Uncle tells me that if you had not stopped the horse, nothing could have saved us;" and she shuddered slightly.

"I am very thankful, indeed, that I have been permitted to be of service to you," began Benny.

Then Mrs. Munroe came forward, and the conversation drifted off into matters in general, for which he was very thankful, and ended in Eva being requested to sing.

"What are your favourite songs?" asked Mrs. Munroe.

"Well, I hardly know," said Benny, blushing. "I know so very few; but the simpler they are the better they please me, as a rule."

"Could you mention one or two?"

"Yes; there is one called 'Love at Home,' which I like very much."

"Oh, that is one of your old songs, dear," said Mrs. Munroe, turning to Eva. "You remember it, don't you?"

"Yes, quite well; but I don't care to sing it, aunt, unless Mr. Bates very much wishes to hear it."

"I should like to hear it again very much," said Benny; "but don't sing it if you would rather not."

"I will do my best, anyhow;" and she got up and went to the piano.

"Ring for lights, dear," said Mrs. Munroe, addressing her daughter; "it is getting quite dark."

"No, no, aunt, please," said Eva; "I know it quite well without the music, and I think the gloaming is the nicest part of the day;" and she sat down and began to play over the air; then there was a long pause, for Eva's thoughts had wandered away elsewhere.

"We are all attention, dear," said Mrs. Munroe.

"Excuse me," said Eva; "but I was thinking of something else. I will tell you all about it directly, if you care to hear."

Then, clear and sweet, rang out the words:

> "There is beauty all around
> When there's love at home."

And Benny felt thankful that the lights had not been brought, for in the gloom he could hide his emotion. When the song was finished, Eva swung herself round on the music-stool, and said, "You will think me very silly, I have no doubt, but I never sing that old song without thinking of what happened years ago."

"Dear me, how old you talk!" laughed her cousin.

"Well, Dot, I *am* getting old; but never mind, I was only a little girl then. Pa and I were returning from Chester, and when we landed from the railway-boat, a pale hungry-looking lad came up to pa and asked him to carry his bag. Well, pa had been delayed, and consequently he was in a hurry, so he said 'No' to the boy in a stern voice, and pushed roughly past, and I saw the boy turn away and begin to cry; so scarcely thinking what I was doing, I went to the boy, and asked him why he cried, and he said he was hungry and cold, that he had no father or mother, and that he had just buried his little sister, and nobody would employ him; so I gave him a new shilling that pa had given me, and asked him if he was generally on the landing-stage.

"'Yes,' he said; and his face brightened wonderfully at the sight of the shilling, and an honest-looking face it was too; 'I'm mostly hereabouts.'

"Well," continued Eva, after a pause, "I thought no more about the lad for several days, when one afternoon I was in the dining-room alone, and I began to play and sing 'Love at Home.' When I had finished, I rose to close the window, and there just outside was the very boy I had given the shilling to, his eyes full of tears; but when he saw he was noticed he shrank away, as if ashamed he had been caught listening."

"And so you conceived a romantic attachment for the lad?" chimed in Mr. Munroe.

"Of course I did, uncle; but to be serious. Teacher had been telling us that we ought to be little missionaries, etc., and I thought this was a likely case to experiment on. So I got pa interested, and in the end the boy was taken into his office, and a better boy pa said he never had. He was honest, truthful, industrious, and seemed very anxious to learn."

Then there was another pause, and if Benny ever felt thankful for the darkness, he did then. It was all clear to him now. This, then, was his little angel, grown into a grand lady! and yet she had not forgotten the poor street boy. He would like to have spoken, and put an end to further revelations, but he dared not trust himself to speak.

Then Eva went on again: "I come now to the most painful part of the story. This boy had been with pa six months, when one Saturday afternoon he left him in charge of the office, but he had scarcely got a hundred yards from the door when he remembered that he had left a bank-note on his desk, and instantly turned back for it. Well, when he got into the office the note was gone.

Nobody had been in the office but the boy, and yet he denied ever having seen it. Well, pa was quite in a way. He searched everywhere, but it was not to be found. So the boy was apprehended on suspicion, and taken to the police-station. I was in a great way, too, for it was through me that pa had employed the boy; still, I could not believe that he was dishonest. At the trial he was given the benefit of the doubt and dismissed, and has never been seen or heard of since. But the strangest part of all is about a month later pa wanted to look at the Directory – a book he does not use very often – and the first thing on which his eye fell as he opened the book was the missing bank-note. He was in a way when he came home, and we chatted about nothing else all the evening, for he remembered then very distinctly how he had laid the note on the open book, and before he went out had shut it up quickly, and placed it on the shelf. What troubled pa so much was, the boy had been robbed of his character, for the magistrates had little doubt of his guilt, though there was no positive evidence; and when a lad's character is gone his fortune is gone. All inquiries concerning him have been fruitless. And pa says sometimes that he feels occasionally as if he had driven the poor boy to destruction. So you see whenever I sing that song it always brings back to my mind this painful story."

After the story was ended there was silence for a few moments. Benny would like to have spoken, but his heart was too full – to think that the shadow was lifted from his life at last! He wished he could have been alone for a few moments, that he might out of the fulness of his heart have thanked God.

"What a pity," said Mrs. Munroe at length, "that the boy could not be found."

Then Benny got up, and said in a voice tremulous with emotion, "I must go now, please; but before I go I would like to say that I am the lost boy."

"You!" they all said in chorus.

"Yes. I cannot say more now." And he sat down again, and hid his face in his hands.

"How strange!" said Eva; "but I see it all now. I could not think who you reminded me of; but you have strangely altered."

"Yes, I suppose I have," he said huskily; "and yet, perhaps, not more than you have."

"How thankful pa will be!" she said, not heeding his last remark. "I will write and tell him tomorrow."

"Well," said Mr. Munroe, speaking at length, "if this is not the strangest ending to a story that I ever came across!"

"It's as good as a novel," said Miss Munroe. "I declare it would make a capital tale."

"And your father is satisfied that I am honest now?" said Benny, going towards Eva.

"Yes; but I don't think that he ever really believed you were dishonest."

"And you never doubted my honesty?"

"No, never."

That was all that passed between them.

When he had gone Mr. Munroe remarked, "A wonderful young man that; I never in my life met with a more remarkable case. How the young fellow has managed to bear up and fight the world as he has is beyond my comprehension."

"And he has the bearing of a gentleman too," remarked Miss Munroe. "I expected we were going to be highly amused at his behaviour and his dialect, and so on; but really he speaks quite correctly."

"He always was a well-behaved boy," remarked Eva; "and during the time he was in pa's office he told one of the clerks that he was very anxious to speak correctly."

"He must have worked very hard, however," said Mr. Munroe; "and a lad with such application, pluck, and determination is sure to get on. I confess I shall watch his future career with great interest."

"But what surprises me most," said Mrs. Munroe, "is the sterling honesty that seems always to have characterised him. As a rule, those street Arabs have the crudest notions of right and wrong."

"He told me once," said Eva, "that he could just remember his mother, who told him to be honest, and truthful, and good; but his little sister Nelly, who died just before I met him, seems to have been his safeguard, and but for her he said he felt certain he should have been a thief."

Meanwhile the subject of this conversation was making his way along the silent lanes that lay between Brooklands and Scout Farm like one in a dream. Could it be really true, he mused, that he had seen his angel face to face, that he had listened again while she sang "Love at Home," and that he had heard from her own lips how the lost bank-note had been found, and how that now no stain rested upon his name? What a wonderful day it had been! Could it be possible that his long-buried hopes might be realised at last?

In a lonely part of the road he paused and listened, but no sound broke the stillness. Above him twinkled the silent stars; around him all nature lay hushed and still.

"God is here," he said; and lifting up his face to the sky, and clasping his hands together, he poured out his heart in thanksgiving.

"O God!" he said, "I thank Thee for all things; for the sorrow, and pain, and loss, for the darkness through which I have wandered, and for the burdens I have had to bear. Thou hast never forsaken me. Thou hast always been good. I thank Thee for bringing me here, and for the discipline of toil. And now that Thou hast lifted off the cloud that so long has darkened my life, help me to praise Thee, and love Thee more and more. I want to be good, and noble, and true. Help me, O Father, for Thy mercy's sake."

Benny slept but little that night. In the long silent hours he lived all his life over again, and wondered at the mercy of God.

CHAPTER XXIII

The Question Settled

Life's withered leaves grew green again and fresh with
childhood's spring,
As I am welcomed back once more within its rainbow ring;
The past, with all its gathered charms, beckons me back in joy,
And loving hearts and open arms re-clasp me as a boy.

Massey

NEXT morning Benny was unusually quiet, so much so that Mrs. Fisher thought he was not well; but he insisted that nothing was the matter with him, and she did not like to question him further. But when Mr. Fisher came in to breakfast he began to rally Benny at once, and to ask him how he got on with the grand folks on the previous evening.

"Very well, I think," Benny answered, simply; "they all seemed very grateful for the little service I had been able to render them,"

"And did you find the ladies lions, Benny?" inquired Mrs. Fisher.

"Indeed no," said Benny, colouring; "they all of them made me think more of angels than of lions."

"Indeed?" said Mrs. Fisher, in a questioning tone.

"Yes, they treated me with the utmost kindness, every one of them; but, now I think of it, the ladies always have done so," said Benny, with a laugh.

"I should think so," interposed Mr. Fisher; "but Mr. Munroe spoke to me about helping you in some way: did he say anything to you about it?"

"Yes; that was what he wanted to see me at his house for principally."

"Well, lad, out with it: did he make you an offer of some sort?"

"Yes, he made me a very kind offer indeed."

"Well, Ben, what was it like? You are precious slow this morning."

"Am I?"

"You are, indeed. He hasn't proposed suicide to you, has he?"

"Not quite. But I had better tell you all that passed between us."

"Of course you accepted his offer?" said Mr. Fisher, when he had done.

"No, I did not."

"You didn't?"

"No; I said I would like to talk to you about it before coming to a decision."

"You needn't fear, lad," said Mr. Fisher, with a little shake in his voice, "that I will put a straw in your way. I shall be very sorry to lose you, I confess, for you have been a great help to me, especially as neither Harry nor George would take to farming, and I know you have been a great comfort to the missus."

"That he has," said Mrs. Fisher, as if speaking to herself.

"But," continued Mr. Fisher, without heeding his wife's remark, "I have thought for some time past that you might do better for yourself than slaving on a farm all the days of your life; and now that you've got the chance of bettering your condition, my advice is, accept it by all means, and think yourself a lucky dog for getting such an offer."

"Oh, yes, Benny," said Mrs. Fisher, "I think you had better accept Mr. Munroe's offer: such a chance does not often come twice in a lifetime; and besides, you can still make this your home – that is, you will be able to come on a Saturday night and stay until Monday morning."

"Of course you will, Ben; I never thought of that," said Mr. Fisher. "I believe you have got into luck's way at last."

"But I have something more to tell you yet," said Benny, looking up with a smile.

"More in the way of good luck?" said Mr. Fisher.

"Well, I don't think the word luck will apply exactly, and yet what I have to tell you is to me very good news indeed."

"Well, lad, out with it: you are beating about the bush in tremendous style this morning, and no mistake."

"Oh, you are so impatient!" laughed Benny; "and I declare you look a great deal more curious than Mrs. Fisher does."

"Well, and what has that to do with it, you tantalising young vagabond?"

"Oh, a great deal!" said Benny, laughing: "you always profess that curiosity is a feminine weakness which you are a stranger to, and yet here you are as curious and impatient as a schoolgirl!" and Benny laughed again.

"Well, Ben," laughed Mr. Fisher, "you have me this time, I'll admit. I am a bit curious, there's no denying it; so let us know what this piece of good news is."

"You have heard me speak," said Benny, "of the little girl that gave me my lucky shilling years ago?"

"The angel, you mean, Benny," said Mrs. Fisher, with a smile.

"Yes, that's who I mean," said Benny, blushing; "and I am not quite certain that she is not an angel yet."

"Well, and what of her?" said Mr. Fisher.

"I daresay you will think it a strange story, but it seems she is a niece of Mr. Munroe, and is staying at present at Brooklands. She was with Mr. Munroe the night the horse took fright, and so without knowing it I saved the life of the little girl that befriended me in the hour of my greatest need. A little girl no longer, however, for she has grown into a grand lady, and yet she seems as good and kind as ever."

"Well, I never!" said Mr. Fisher.

"And you recognised each other at once?" inquired his wife.

"No, that we didn't: she has grown out of recollection quite; and I suppose I have also."

"Well, I should rather think you have," said Mr. Fisher, with a broad grin; "you were a scarecrow when you found your way here, and no mistake."

"But how did you find out who she was?" said Mrs. Fisher.

"By the merest accident. But you would never guess, so I will tell you all about it." And he detailed the circumstances with which the reader is familiar.

"Well, if I ever!" grunted Mr. Fisher.

"I'm so thankful, Benny," Mrs. Fisher remarked; "though the finding of the note can make no difference in our regard for you, for we never doubted your honesty for a moment."

"Thank you, mammy;" and he looked fondly up into the face of the good woman who for so many years had been as a mother to him.

After breakfast Benny took a book and went out into the fields to read, but somehow today the letters got hopelessly mixed, and all the lines seemed to run into one. He did his best to fix his mind upon the subject of the book, but in vain: before he had read a dozen words the letters would fade away, and his thoughts would be somewhere else; and not only his thoughts, but his eyes kept wandering in the direction of Brooklands, and he found himself weaving all kinds of fancies. But in every pattern stood out the face of one he had never forgotten either in joy or pain. How grandly life was opening out before him again! The mountain heights that had been so long in darkness were once more bathed in light. The wilderness surely lay all behind him now. Ah! he had thought so once before, and had found out that he had only just commenced the journey across the dreary waste. Was it to be so again? Would this glorious morning close in darkness? Were hopes always delusive, and but the prelude of despair? He knew not; and yet he had no fear. "The Lord," he said, "has always provided for me; I believe He always will."

Then a lark rose up from its lowly nest near him, and went singing upward through the sky, and as he listened to the full rich song that floated down to him, he seemed to hear in it the promise of an ever-faithful Friend – "And not one of them falls to the ground without the notice of His eye … Are ye not much better than they?"

Towards the close of the afternoon Benny found himself in the lane that led down to the bridge that crossed the dell. He had no particular object in view, only he loved a quiet stroll through the country lanes in the quiet of the day, and he was useless on the farm till his arm got better. Below in the valley the river rippled pleasantly over its stony bed. To Benny's ears it sounded like a song, while his own fancy supplied the words:

"There is beauty all around
When there's love at home."

On turning the sharp corner of which we have already spoken, he came suddenly face to face with Eva Lawrence. Benny blushed scarlet; but Eva held out her hand in a simple childish manner, and said frankly, "I am pleased to see you ..." (she was about to say "Benny," but checked herself), and added, "I hope your arm is still improving."

"Yes, thank you; it will soon be as well as ever."

"I am very glad; but how strange, isn't it, that I should have found you again?"

"Yes, very; but my life has been a strange one altogether."

"I suppose so. Do you remember telling me all about your life up to the time I first saw you on the landing-stage?"

"Yes, I remember. Do you remember giving me the shilling? Of course you do, for you mentioned it last night, but I wanted to tell you I have that shilling yet."

And Benny took the shilling out of his purse and handed it to her.

"How funny!" said she, taking the coin in her hand; "and is this the very same?"

"Yes; I have never had the heart to part with it, somehow, though I've wanted bread since you gave it to me. I call it my lucky shilling."

"How strange!" she said, more to herself than to him. "Then you have never forgotten us?"

"Forgotten you!" said Benny, "I should ..." Then he checked himself, and added, after a pause, "No, I could not easily forget those who have befriended me."

By this time they had reached the bridge, and Eva sat down on the low parapet, and Benny took a seat opposite her. For a while neither spoke, then Eva looked up and said, "Would you mind telling me about yourself since that dreadful evening you had to leave pa's office?"

"If you care to hear it, though I fear it would be a very uninteresting story."

"I should like to hear it very much, for I have often wondered what could have become of you."

"I should not have kept silence all these years if I had thought anyone cared to know what had become of me, but I supposed that I should best please those who had known me by keeping out of their sight."

"You were mistaken in that, I am sure; but never mind now, I am all curiosity to hear your story."

Benny could not resist this request, so he gave her an outline of what we have given in greater detail, making as little as possible, however, of his sufferings and privations, and dwelling at length, and with much feeling, on the kindness of his friends at the farm. Of his inner life he said nothing. His religious experience seemed too deep for words, too sacred for parade, and he had not framed an experience yet to use on public occasions, and he preferred also that his actions, rather than his words, should reveal his religious life.

Eva listened with great attention, and her quick imagination supplied what she felt he had left out. For a while there was silence after Benny had told his story, save for the clear river that babbled down underneath the bridge, for both were thinking of the old days that had passed away for ever.

At length Eva arose and held out her hand, and Benny took the little white fingers in his hard brown palm, and held them just for a moment.

"Good evening, Mr. Bates; I must go home now," she said.

"Good evening, Miss Lawrence." And Benny watched her glide away among the shadows of the tall trees, in the direction of Brooklands, then turned and walked slowly home.

The next morning, as he was leaving the house, he almost stumbled over Mr. Lawrence, who on receipt of his daughter's letter had come over at once.

"Mr. Lawrence!" said Benny, in a tone of surprise.

"Then you are Benny, I suppose," he said, "as you recognise me, but I should never have known you."

"Yes, I am Benny Bates, but you have not altered in the least; I should have known you anywhere."

"Well, Benny," said Mr. Lawrence with much feeling, taking his hand, "you cannot tell how thankful I am to see you alive and well." Then, glancing at Benny's arm, which he still carried in a sling, he added, "I beg pardon, I had forgotten your arm for a moment. I have to thank you also for saving my daughter's life."

"Do not mention it, Mr. Lawrence; I have received abundant thanks already."

"That may be, but I have much to say to you; can you spare time for a walk?"

"Yes, with pleasure; I am able to do nothing, as you see, and so time hangs rather heavy."

"Benny," said Mr. Lawrence, when they had gone some distance, "when I found that missing bank-note, I resolved that, if ever I saw you again or had the chance of speaking to you, I would ask your forgiveness for the wrong I did you."

"Do not speak in that way, please," said Benny. "If you wronged me it was not intentionally, so that I have nothing to forgive; if I had, it should be freely granted."

"Thank you. And now, Benny, will you return to Liverpool again? Not to be office boy," he said, glancing at Benny's tall and well-knit frame; "I can find you something much better than that, and I should like to make you some

211

reparation for all you have suffered through me."

"Thank you, Mr. Lawrence," said Benny firmly; "but I could not come simply to be tolerated because you fancied you had wronged me, and wished to make amends."

Mr. Lawrence looked up in surprise.

"You will understand what I mean, I think," said Benny. "I am too old and too big to be any longer an object of charity, but if you think I am able to fill the place you want filled, and am worth the salary that you are in the habit of paying, then I will consider your very kind proposal."

"I understand what you mean now," said Mr. Lawrence, "and I must say I admire your independence. I do not wish you to be an object of charity, for Mr. Munroe tells me that he finds, through inquiries that he has made, that you are a good pen-man, and quick at accounts, and if you will come and take the vacant stool in my office, I shall be sincerely obliged."

"Thank you; but do you know that Mr. Munroe has made me a similar offer?"

"Yes."

"Do you require an answer now?"

"To-morrow will do."

"Let it be to-morrow, then, please, and I will think about it in the meanwhile."

Benny had decided the question, however, before he slept that night. Manchester was a strange place; Liverpool was his home. He knew every street for half a mile around the Custom House as well as he knew the lanes around Scout Farm. He had spent his childhood there; his earliest, ay, and his happiest recollections were associated with it. It had been the scene of his greatest struggles and triumphs. It had witnessed his deepest joy and his bitterest sorrow, and though he had left it in disgrace and pain, he loved it still.

There were a few people there he had pined to see. It was Joe Wrag's home; it was Nelly's resting-place; granny lived there, and his Sunday-school teacher, and Mr. Lawrence, and – But never mind, Liverpool was dear to him still, and in the very spot from which he had been driven in disgrace he would start afresh.

Next morning he walked across to Brooklands, and asked to see Mr. Munroe.

"I have come," he said, as soon as that gentleman appeared, "to tell you that I cannot accept your very kind offer."

"I guessed as much," said Mr. Munroe, with a smile, "when I heard Mr. Lawrence had been after you. So Liverpool has more attractions for you than Manchester, eh?"

"Yes, sir, Liverpool is my home, and Manchester would be strange to me; but I am very much obliged to you for your kindness."

"I do not blame you, Mr. Bates; on the contrary, I think you have acted wisely. Still, if at any time you should need a friend, you may reckon upon me."

"Thank you, sir," said Benny, with a shake in his voice, "thank you very much; and now, sir, could I see Mr. Lawrence?"

"Oh, yes, I will send him to you at once."

"Good morning, Benny," was Mr. Lawrence's greeting; "and have you settled the matter?"

"Yes, sir, I will accept your offer."

"That's right; I am glad to hear it. And now, when can you be ready?"

"In a week, sir."

"That will do; and in the meantime I will secure lodgings for you, and make things as straight and pleasant against your arrival as I possibly can."

"Thank you very much."

"Don't name it; but I will send you word when I have secured a comfortable home for you, so that if you like to send on your luggage beforehand, you may do so."

The next few days Benny was busy getting his things together, previous to his departure from Scout Farm. Little Winnie followed him everywhere, and wanted him to promise her that he would not "do away". He did not think until he began to pack his things that the parting would cost him so much, nor did he know till then how closely the little prattling Winnie had twined herself around his heart.

"Benny does not 'ove his 'ittle Winnie, to do away," the child repeated over and over again, with choking voice and brimming eyes.

"Benny's pet," he would say, taking her up in his arms and kissing away her tears; "he loves you more than he can tell."

"Then Benny'll stay with Winnie, won't he?"

"Do you want Benny to stay very badly, eh, pet?"

"Oh, yes, Winnie 'oves 'oo werry much; don't do away, Benny."

"I'll come back again at Christmas, Winnie, and then we'll have rare fun, and I'll bring you a new doll and heaps of oranges."

But the child would not be comforted.

At length the last morning of his stay arrived. It was a silent party that sat down to breakfast, for the hearts of all were too full for speech. Then the trap was brought round, and they all drove over to the station together. The train was in time this morning, for which Benny felt thankful. There was only time for a hurried good bye, an extra kiss for Winnie, and the train started for the busy town where Benny was to commence afresh the race of life.

CHAPTER XXIV

The Reward of Well-Doing

I have seen angels in the gloomy prison,
In crowded halls, by the lone widow's hearth;
And when they passed the fallen have uprisen,
The giddy paused, the mourner's hope had birth.

And by his side there moved a form of beauty,
Strewing sweet flowers along his path of life,
And looking up with meek and love-lent duty:
I call her angel, but he called her wife.

ON reaching Liverpool, his first visit was to his sister's grave. He would never have found it, were it not for a curious-shaped stone that he had embedded in the sod ere he went away. As it was, he was a long time before he could discover it among the hundreds of grass-grown mounds lying all around it. It seemed to him that he had lived a long life since he lay there that summer night, and resolved that he would leave Liverpool behind him, and go out into the great world that lay beyond to seek his fortune.

"Ah, well!" he mused, "I have made no fortune, but I have lived a life of peace, and God has taken care of me, and now I have come back again no longer a child, though scarcely a man, and I believe God will take care of me here." Kneeling by the little grave, he offered up a silent prayer for help and protection. He thanked God for his little sister that was safe from the world's temptation, and prayed that when he should be laid down to sleep by her side, they might meet by the far-off Jordan river, and part no more for ever.

He was in a very subdued frame of mind when he left the cemetery and wended his way in the direction of Tempest Court. He could not help wondering as he threaded his way through the busy streets whether granny was still alive, but he certainly did not expect to find that Tempest Court was no longer in existence. Such, however, was the case. The march of improvement had swept away hundreds of tumble-down houses, in one of which granny had dwelt for so many years. But she did not live to see that day. In the little home in which she had lived so long she was permitted to die; and so, when the 'destroyer', as she would have called it, came to Tempest Court, she was gone – gone home to the Father's mansion, to the "house not made with hands, eternal in the heavens."

But Benny knew nothing of this, and so he gazed with a look of pain at the heaps of broken bricks and mortar which men were busy carting away, and thought what a grief it would be to granny. His next visit was to St. George's Hall, and for a while he sat in the shadow of the great portico to watch the hurrying crowds passing up and down. How different it was from the silent country and the still, drowsy fields! What a tremendous hurry everybody seemed to be in! Was it always so? He had never noticed it in the old days: surely the great town must have grown bigger and busier in the years he had been away from it. "But I daresay I shall soon get used to it," he said to himself, as he rose from his seat, and started this time for the landing-stage. Here he saw no change. The mighty river was the same as in the old days, a scene of life and beauty. But the children selling matches and the women crying newspapers brought more vividly back to his mind than anything else the days of his own childhood. In the cemetery it seemed a life-time since he went away; here, on the stage, it seemed only yesterday since he was a poor famished child, earning a precarious living as best he could. He could hardly realise that he was a strong, well-dressed young man. Once or twice the word "Perks" leaped to his lips as a shock-headed ragged lad ran against him; and when a little girl came up to him with "Fusees, sir?" the face of his dead little sister seemed to flash upon him for a moment, and he started and turned pale, then handed the child some coppers, and patted her on the head, telling her to be a good girl.

He now began to think it time to put in an appearance at Mr. Lawrence's office. But he could not resist the temptation of a sail to Birkenhead and back first. For years he had longed for the day when he would be rich enough to afford such a luxury; that day had come at last, and the wish should be gratified; and surely, as he floated across the broad placid river and back again, no child ever felt half so delighted with a new toy as did he.

Mr. Lawrence was pleased to see that our hero had arrived, and offered him the option of a few days' holiday before he settled down to the desk. But Benny said he would be quite ready for work on the following morning; he only wanted to see Joe Wrag and granny, and he thought he would be able to find them before the day closed, and he knew that he should be happier at work than doing nothing.

Benny's next move was to make inquiries of the police as to what streets were being repaired; and, having been furnished with a list, he waited until half-past five, and then went in search of his old friend. But Joe was not so easily found as he had imagined. He went from one street to another until his list was exhausted; but all the watchmen were strangers to him, and he began to fear that his old friend was either dead, or that failing health and strength had compelled him to retire from his occupation. Benny now began to consider what he was to do next, for he had not the remotest idea in what part of the town Joe lived, if indeed he were still living.

At length it occurred to him that very likely the watchmen knew each other, and that if he were to inquire of one of them he might get some idea of Joe's whereabouts. With Benny to think was to act very frequently; so he walked up to an old man who was keeping watch in the street in which he then found himself, and put the question at once.

"Do you know an old man by the name of Joe Wrag?"

"Oh, ay, very well."

"Then perhaps you could tell me where I might find him."

"In course I could. If you keep down Old Hall Street for haaf a mile, you'll tumble over him, unless yer mind where yer goin'."

"Much obliged." And off Benny started with a very much lighter heart than he had five minutes before. It was a warm July evening, and Benny espied the old man long before he got to him, sitting on a block of wood outside his hut, apparently buried in thought.

For a moment or two Benny stood before him without speaking, and Joe seemed utterly unconscious of his presence. Six years seemed to have passed very lightly over the old man's head. Benny could detect no change in his features; he did not look a day older than he did the last time he saw him.

At length Benny said, in a hesitating tone of voice, "Good evening, Mr. Wrag."

Joe started, but scarcely lifted his eyes to the intruder; then answered, after a pause, "I'm none so much mister, as I knows on; I'm only plain Joe Wrag."

"This is a nice time of the year for you watch-men," said Benny, not knowing exactly what to say.

"Yes, it's purty fair; we don't git bothered quite so much wi' the youngsters as we do in the winter."

"And so the children bother you in the winter, do they?"

"Well, I don't know they bother me so much, arter all; only they like the fire, yer see, when' the weather's cold."

"Just so; you'll get to know a great many children, I should think?"

"Oh, ay, a goodish few."

"Did you ever know a lad called Benny Bates?"

"Ay, yes, poor lad, I should think I did," said Joe, with a sigh; "an' his little sister too, purty little hangel; she's safe enough, thank God. She's wi' the Lord in heaven, but where the poor lad is the Lord only knows."

"Lost, then, is he?"

"Oh, ay, poor bairn, poor persecuted lad; falsely accused he wur, an' it seemed to break his 'eart; he's never been heard of since."

"Do you think you would know him if he were to come back again?"

"Ay, I should know'im among a thousand," said the old man, still keeping his eyes on the ground.

"Then look at me, Joe, and say if you know me."

Instantly he rose to his feet, and, coming close to Benny, looked straight in his face. Then raising his hands to heaven, he cried out, "O Lord of mercy!" and fell upon Benny's neck and wept.

We will not tire the reader with repeating the conversation that passed between Joe and Benny that night.

Each had a hundred things to say to each other, and each a hundred questions to ask. Darkness had crept over the earth, and the great town was silent and still, ere Benny left Joe's hut; and when at length he took his departure, Joe watched him until he had disappeared in the gloom, then looking up into the now star-lighted sky, he clasped his hands together, while the tears ran down his weatherbeaten cheeks, and cried out "Now, Lord, lettest Thou Thy servant depart in peace, for mine eyes have seen Thy salvation."

Next day Benny settled down to work with a fixed determination to do his duty, and to make his way in the world if it could be honestly done. The same truthfulness and perseverance, and diligence and honesty that had characterised him for so many years still marked his life, and raised him month by month and year by year in the estimation of his employer and in the estimation of all with whom he came in contact. According to promise he spent his Christmas at Scout Farm, to the delight of little Winnie and of all the other members of the household, and returned to town feeling all the better for a week's rest.

When Benny had been in Liverpool about two years, a case that was tried at the assizes created considerable interest. The prisoner was found guilty of burglary and manslaughter, and sentenced to twenty-one years' penal servitude. In reading an account of the trial, Benny was struck with the names of the prisoner, John Cadger, alias Peeler, alias Perks. Could it be the Perks that he had known? So interested was he in this question that he determined to find out if possible; and, after some difficulty he was permitted to visit the prisoner in his cell, previous to his removal to Dartmoor.

Benny's first glance at the shock head and sinister face convinced him that his worst fears were realised. For a moment he was unable to speak, then summoning up all his courage, he held out his hand, saying, "I'm very sorry to see you here, Perks."

"Who are you?" snarled Perks with a terrible oath.

"Do you not know me?" said Benny.

"No! I only know you b'longs to the gentry tribe that are always down on poor chaps like us."

"You are mistaken there, Perks; I am Benny Bates."

"You!" he said in astonishment, eyeing him from head to foot. "Then you must 'ave got mighty 'igh in the perfeshun. I could never dress like that."

"I am not in the profession, as you call it," said Benny.

"Not in it?"

"No."

"Do you mean to say you've kep' honest all these years?"

"Yes, I have."

"An' kep' in Liverpool?"

"No." And Benny told him where he had been.

"Jist so; you'd a-been bound to take up the perfeshun if you'ad kep' here."

"I don't think so."

"I'm sure on it. Look'ere: do you 'member that chat we 'ad that night I skeered yer so? Oh, lor!" And Perks laughed till the tears ran down his face. "Well, Ben, I tried bein' honest after I got out o' quad that time. I did for sure, jist by way of speriment; but lor! 't were no use, – I was nearly starved, 'an I had to take up the bizness agin or else die."

"But why did not you do as I did?"

"Never thought on it, and shouldn't a-'ad pluck enough to hacted it out if I 'ad."

Then Benny talked seriously to Perks about his sin, and about the everlasting future beyond the grave; told him also about a loving Saviour, who was ready to forgive the vilest, and of the happy home He had prepared for all.

Perks listened in silence to all Benny had to say, only remarking when he had finished, "I wish I wur dead."

He confessed to Benny the justice of his sentence, though he would insist upon it that society had made him what he was, and was to some degree responsible for his wickedness.

To Benny the interview was a very painful one, and he felt it a relief when he found himself once more outside the prison walls. They never met again. In less than three years Perks was summoned to appear before a higher tribunal, to answer for the deeds done in the body.

Benny had no sooner got settled in Liverpool than he sought out his old Sunday school, and became a teacher there; and often he told to the ragged and neglected children that he gathered around him the story of his life, and pointed out a bright future that might be theirs if they would be industrious, truthful, and honest. Once during each summer he made it a point of taking his class to Eastham Woods, knowing from his own experience what a joy it would be to the poor boys to breathe the fresh air, listen to the song of birds, and run races on the mossy sward. Benny was never idle. The one aim of his life was to do good, to be "rich in good works;" and grandly he succeeded. His name in many a home was like "ointment poured forth," and young and old blessed him for his kindly words and kindlier deeds.

✳✳✳✳✳

And now what shall we more say? for tales must end while lives run on. Years – I need not say how many – have passed away since Benny again took up his abode in Liverpool. He is now partner with Mr. Lawrence, in a business that has become more prosperous than ever. He lives in a beautiful house of his own, and the angel that years ago brightened his childhood now brightens his home; and sometimes on winter evenings he gathers his children around his knee, and shows them a shilling still bright and little worn, and tells them how their mother gave it to him when she was a little girl, and he a poor, ragged, starving boy upon the streets; tells them how, by being honest, truthful, and persevering, he had worked his way through many difficulties, and how, by the blessing and mercy of God, he had been kept until that day. And Ben, the eldest lad, thinks how he will be brave and true like his father, and so grow up to be an honourable man.

Here, then, we will end our story – a story that contains more truth than fiction – and hope that the young people who may read it may learn the lesson we have aimed to teach, and so be helped to the cultivation of those virtues that will yield them in this world "a hundredfold more, and in the world to come life everlasting."

THE END